CORVETTE

FIRST COMMAND

Starship Series: 1

By

Ken McConnell

GB PRESS

CORVETTE First Command
Starship Series: 1

Paperback ISBN: 978-1-969784-06-4

Second Edition: February 2026

Cover Art: Byron McConnell

Chapter 1

J ace Linder was the first human to step onto the distant planet. After leaping off the lander's platform, he turned around and immediately saw the deep indentations of human footprints. How was that possible? He was the only person to egress the ship. No one had ever been this far outside of known space before.

"Are you down, Jace?" came the concerned voice of Elle from inside the lander.

Jace was too stunned to reply. Finally, he muttered. "Yeah, but someone has beaten us here."

"What? Say again?"

"There are footprints everywhere, leading off to a rock formation directly south."

There was a long silence from inside the ship. Jace bent down to record the impressions in the fine, verdant granules of the planet's surface. They had informally named the planet Jade based on how green the features were from space. Orbital scans indicated high concentrations of iron and actinolite, a green silicate. Up close, the sandy material resembled volcanic beaches on the more hospitable planets of the Federation.

The large sandy crystals left footprints that were not as detailed as in lunar dust. There were no noticeable boot treads or other markings—just a trail of several human-looking prints strolling across the landing site. The lander's engine had kicked up the sand under it and erased some of the prints. Jace moved around the lander, checking the outside for any signs of distress from the landing. He found it in perfect shape and saw the footprints again on the exact opposite side of the lander. It looked like they stretched forever over the dull green surface.

He was in a full pressure suit as it was impossible to be outside without a breather mask and way colder than the Arctic regions of most planets.

"Hey, I'm gonna follow these prints for a while, see if I can tell where they go," Jace said.

Elle sternly warned: "Don't go out of sight until someone can join you. "

She was the Second Officer of the ship and the ground team's leader. One other crewman was in the lander—Macy Owens—waiting to egress in the airlock.

"I'm coming out," she said, pushing the manual outer latch open. She scampered down the short ladder to the surface and immediately bent down to trace the footsteps with her gloved index finger.

"Hard to say, but I think they may even have been made recently." She looked up to see Jace waving at her to follow him.

"Come on, I think I see where they were heading," Jace said.

Macy hopped along in giant strides on the tiny planet's less than one G gravity. She caught up quickly and came to a stop beside him. They looked out over a small ravine shadowed by a jagged rock outcrop from the nearby foothills. There were twisted metallic objects scattered on the furrowed ground as if something had crashed.

Jace held up an arm to stop Macy from heading to the site.

"We don't want to risk puncturing our suits. Maybe we should send a drone," Jace said.

Macy shook her head inside her helmet. "It would take too long to drag it out and launch it. Let's proceed slowly."

Jace took smaller steps, with Macy following him at a few paces. Both looked around carefully to make sure they didn't miss anything important. The metal pieces were all smaller than an arm's length; many were as green as the sand on one side and a blue-gray color on the inside.

As they got closer, they saw a tubular-shaped object resembling an old-fashioned rocket. The frequency of footprints increased all around the cylinder. It looked like whatever crashed had been picked over by someone. Parts of the cylinder were removed and randomly tossed aside.

"Scavengers, maybe?" Macy asked.

"More likely some kind of search and recovery team."

Macy bent over the conical front of the cylinder and pointed. "Looks like some kind of cockpit."

Jace looked away from the site in a sweeping scan for his suit camera, partly to record the scene and partly out of alarm. He half expected whoever had picked over this site to return.

"Do you think it was pirates?" Jace asked. He was concerned that if it were pirates, they had no real defenses; they were explorers, not the military.

Macy stood back up and turned over a piece of green metal with her boot. It was shiny on the other side and covered in a printed text she didn't recognize.

"I don't think this was a pirate ship, and I don't think it was human either," Macy said.

Jace switched to the intercom on his transmitter so only Macy could hear him. "I knew we should have examined the landing zone closer. We would have noticed this wreck," he said.

Macy nodded inside her helmet as she stood up. The sky was an eerie yellow color except for the greenish glow of the star in the sky. The star was not green, but it took on a light emerald color between the heavy air and the green stellar gases nearby. She caught herself staring at the sky just as a flash of light shone brighter than the stars for a few seconds.

***

Captain Sullivan leaned forward in his chair and peered out the dual windows on the bridge. The thick panes of glass came together in a thin strip of metal an arm's length from where he sat. It offered him a nearly unobstructed view forward into space. The pilot and the science stations were behind and below him. His First Officer, Giles, stood before him, his hands on the cold glass.

They tracked the incoming vessels that zipped past the bridge fast enough to snap their heads.

"What the hell was that?" Sullivan asked rhetorically.

Giles's eyes were wide as full moons. "They looked like attack ships, sir."

Sullivan spun his chair around to face the science station. "Track them," was all he could manage to say.

The ships looked to him exactly like fighter planes from ancient history. They were dark green with yellow leading edges on their wings, and he was sure he had seen guns on them.

The Science Officer was a young woman with blonde hair pulled into a tail and narrow, dark eyes. She slipped on headphones and tweaked her scanners. After a few seconds, she slid off the headphones and looked up at the captain.

"Sir, they are coming around for another pass. I don't have any other contacts in this system."

Both Sullivan and Giles went back to the windows to try to see them again. Two blue streaks from the ship's engines led back to some point ahead of them before they turned into the path of the *SS Wayfinder*.

"Mr. Giles, I don't like the look of this," Sullivan muttered.

Giles nodded as he waited impatiently for another pass of the sleek alien ships. Sullivan looked down at the emergency buoy button on his armrest panel. He slid the protective cover off and hovered his hand over it. They were a civilian exploration ship on the farthest fringes of known space. They didn't have any weapons or much in the way of shielding. If those ships were hostile, his crew was as good as dead.

"Captain, they're firing on us!" Giles shouted.

Sullivan slammed his palm over the ejection button and watched helplessly as the expanding bursts of energy engulfed his ship.

***

"Both of you get your asses back here. Something terrible has happened!"

It was the panicked voice of Elle from the lander. They bounced back to the lander as quickly as they could without falling. Macy scrambled up the lander and entered the airlock first. Jace jammed his way inside the airlock after she had cycled through.

Inside the lander, Jace found both women huddled around the comms. Elle was frantically calling the base ship, her voice cracking with fear, while Macy sat stunned by her side, still in her pressure suit.

"What's wrong?" Jace asked.

Macy looked over at him with watering eyes. "They aren't answering. It's as if they're not there anymore. I saw a flash from orbit. Do you think they had a core meltdown?"

"No, they would have contacted us if they had had an emergency."

Jace moved to his seat and started activating their scanners. He pointed them at the orbital position of the *SS Wayfinder* and waited for a return ping. Nothing came. The scanners returned no contacts. He widened the band and tried again—still nothing.

"Oh my God," Macy breathed.

She looked out of her window. The others crowded next to her and watched the brilliant light show of their mothership breaking apart in low orbit. All of them watched open-mouthed as they each realized they were as good as dead.

Elle looked down first, her head awash in anguish for those she knew on the ship. Then she realized they didn't have enough supplies on the lander to last more than a few days.

Macy and Jace slowly looked at eat other and instinctively hugged tightly. They'd been an item even before this latest mission to the farthest reaches of space. The motion detector alarms sounded, startling everyone. Something was moving outside the ship. Elle moved to the only window that looked down and saw nothing.

"Jace, get out there and see what's setting them off. Maybe it's another lander," Elle said.

Jace gave Macy a goodbye peck and then headed back into the airlock. It only took a few minutes to cycle through. Elle reached the comm panel and switched the suit intercom to a speaker.

"Jace, what do you see?" Macy asked. Elle noticed the strain in her voice.

He didn't respond immediately, and she was about to ask again when he replied, "I don't see anything near us. I'm heading to the top of the ridge. Maybe someone has come back for that wreck."

"Be careful!" Macy blurted out.

"I will. Hey, some people are milling about. I," the transmission cut out.

"Jace!" Macy shouted. She locked eyes with Elle, and Elle could see the fear in them.

"He's fine; give him a second to report."

They waited five seconds before Elle contacted him again. "Jace, this is Elle. What do you see?"

There was no response, just dead air.

"I'm going out there," Macy said as she donned her helmet and headed into the airlock. Elle started to protest but realized it was futile. She was going, no matter what Elle said.

Macy dropped down onto the alien planet's surface and immediately brought up her hands. Three black-clad humans surrounded her in pressure suits. They were carrying short swords and some kind of rifle. One of the figures waved his arm, and Macy felt something puncture her suit and her neck. Death came quickly for her as the nearest figure dispatched her with his sword.

Inside the lander, Elle saw a red spray of blood and Macy's helmet roll past her view. Terrified, she started crying as she activated the lander's takeoff routine. The lander shook with an explosion, and the airlock hatch opened unexpectedly behind her. A dark, helmeted figure emerged holding a pistol. Elle's lungs strained and her eyes bulged as she realized the airlock was wide open to the planet's surface. The helmet drew closer, and she could see a blue-faced man inside right before her chest exploded in pain.

Chapter 2

Lieutenant Armon Vance stared out the double-pane observation window at the gray starship to which he was reporting for duty. It was a small, older model Corvette used by the fleet to escort shipping convoys through the pirate-infested space lanes of the Outer Rim. It was the worst possible assignment he could have landed. Lording over a star dinghy at the edge of civilized space. Boring and horribly remote.

Clearly, there had been an administrative snafu, or he was the butt of a terrible prank. His orders were very specific, though. He was to take civilian transportation to Allifax Way Station and report for duty to Captain Xander on the *SS Weippe*. He had looked up the man and the ship on the long voyage to Allifax and nearly wept when he learned his captain was as old as the ship, and both of them were likely to be put out to pasture sooner rather than later.

Vance studied the weathered hull of the Corvette with a mixture of regret and mild interest. The *Weippe* was, in fact, the oldest vessel in the Federation Fleet. Years of duty in space had left her hull pockmarked by interstellar impacts, and her paint faded from exposure to an untold number of stars. His eyes were drawn to the single railgun turret on the vessel. It was twice the size of any ordinary Corvette's gun and looked like a six- or eight-inch double barrel that was usually fitted to a Destroyer. Vance shook his head at the obscenely out-of-place main gun. *It's just another odd blemish on an ancient, ugly boat.*

Sighing, he descended the entry gangway that led to the ship's airlock. His duffel bag hung low around his black service coat in the prescribed manner from the Fleet Officer's Handbook. Vance was all about doing things by the book, even when his station in life was about to be lowered to the bottom rung. His uniform was ship-shape, regardless of his annoyance level or where the Fleet sent him; in this case, to the sticks of the galaxy.

As the airlock slid open to allow him access to the ship, his nose caught a whiff of hot metal - the unmistakable smell of space itself. You only smelled it in the airlocks and shuttle bays of older starships. It just added insult to injury for him as he stepped onto the rust bucket that would be his home for the following year.

A woman came to attention at the duty officer's stand and rendered a perfect salute. She was younger than he was but not by much. Dark eyes and short brown hair. Her gray duty uniform was pressed and clean. He raised an eyebrow as he returned her salute. *Maybe this assignment wouldn't be as bad as he thought.*

"Welcome aboard the *Weippe*, Lieutenant. I'm Sub-Lieutenant Lestor, the officer of the deck."

She extended a hand with a grip that was firm but not tight.

"Captain Xander is waiting for you in his berth. Would you like an escort, sir?"

Vance shook his head. "I can manage. Carry on," he said a bit dismissively.

She returned to her station and crossed him off the boarding list. Several enlisted ratings were coming down the gangway, and her attention was diverted to them.

Vance headed down the narrow corridor leading to the ship's bow. Fleet starships were divided into three main sections: forward, where most officers lived. The body where the rest of the crew lived and where most of the ship's mass was concentrated and the drive section. The forward and the drive sections were separated from the main body by girders and narrow corridors. This was tradition due to the explosive nature of the early stardrives, which were nuclear at the time of the *Weippe's* christening. Modern starships continued to be built in sections to help with cooling and save weight.

***

The corridors of the Corvette were narrow and smelled of paint, chemical cleaners, and the sweat of passing enlisted crewmen. Showering on board a military starship was still considered a luxury, and the enlisted had to endure every other day rotations to conserve water. Officers were on a similar rotation but didn't work as strenuously and tended not to smell as bad. As he made his way through the body and down the starboard access tube to the forward section, he couldn't help but notice the worn metal floors and exposed access panels everywhere. This ship was over fifty years old and showed every crease and line like the face of a dignified elderly woman.

By the time he reached the port side of the main deck, the traffic flow of enlisted crew and construction workers from the dock had thinned out. This was officer's country, and only officers and stewards were allowed on this deck. He found the thin metal hatch of the captain's cabin and rapped three times with his knuckles.

"Come in, Number One," came a fatherly-sounding voice.

Vance wondered how he knew who it was at his door with no window but decided it was probably just a good guess on his part. He likely wasn't bothered much while in port with only a skeleton crew aboard.

Entering the tiny cabin, Vance stood at attention and saluted.

"Lieutenant Armon Vance reporting for duty, sir."

The Captain was an older man with a full gray beard, prominent forehead, and straight nose on his wide, pale face. His eyes were steel gray spheres, alert and knowing—the eyes of a man who had spent his whole life in the black of space. He was reclining in his chair with his arms folded.

Another man stood at ease in the tiny cabin. He was tall, with salt - and - pepper black hair and a pencil-thin mustache. Vance thought he looked familiar but could not put a name to the face.

Captain Xander waved a return salute and pointed to the other man. "This is Lieutenant Commander Ganner, your predecessor."

Vance nodded curtly to the man, who just smiled knowingly as if he knew damn well what Vance was in for working with Xander.

"Good to meet you, Commander," Vance said.

"Likewise, I'm sure. Well, Captain, I best be pushing off and getting to my next assignment," Ganner said, pulling himself up straight.

Xander glanced at Vance. "He's taking the helm of the *Lysander*."

"Outstanding, sir," Vance lied. That's the ship he thought for sure he was going to get. A bigger, sleeker Destroyer bound for the inner core, no doubt.

Xander and Ganner clasped hands warmly.

"Fair winds and a following sea," Xander grinned.

"Thank you, sir. Same to you both," Ganner replied, squeezing past Vance to leave.

Vance didn't exactly know what the old sailor phrase meant, but he would look it up when he had a moment. In the meantime, he shut the door and remained at attention.

Ganner looked him over for a moment and then directed him to take a seat on the bunk. "At ease, Number One," he said.

Vance sat down but was anything but relaxed. Despite the unwanted circumstances, he wanted to make a good impression with his new captain.

"Have you looked her over yet?" Xander asked.

"Not as such, sir."

Xander returned his attention to his display screen. It was filled with documents layered on top of one another. "I want you to walk her every inch and become as familiar as you can with her. We'll meet for dinner in the wardroom when the rest of the staff come aboard. You can be on your way unless you have anything for me."

"No, sir," Vance said, standing at attention again.

"Oh, and change into your duty uniform. We don't wear our blacks in space. Dismissed."

"Aye, sir."

Vance left the captain's cabin and headed to his berth, just a few paces away, to change.

***

In airlock one of the *Weippe*, more officers were reporting for duty with the officer of the day. Lieutenant Lestor welcomed a roguishly pretty sub-lieutenant named Boxer and a thin and pale midshipman named Layton.

"Welcome aboard the *Weippe*. I'll see you both to your quarters," Lestor offered.

Neither of the newcomers refused her offer.

"First time in a Corvette for you both?" she asked.

"First time in the Outer Rim, too. Layton and I were stationed on a Destroyer," Boxer said. Her dark eyes seemed to drink in Lestor, showing she was more than receptive to her. Lestor did her best to ignore the stare.

"The *Weippe* is the oldest ship in the active fleet, but we think she's also the toughest. Her frame and shielding were designed for nuclear drives, so we should have a higher survival rate in combat."

The midshipman Layton spoke with a slightly higher-pitched voice than either woman. "But we're not at war, so that shouldn't matter."

Boxer turned around and looked the shorter man down. "We skirmish with pirates all the time. It's harder for them to get their grapple lines onto us."

Layton nodded his understanding as they all continued single-file down the narrow corridors. When they passed through the connecting tube to the forward section, Lestor guided them to their adjoining bunks.

"You'll share a room with me, Lieutenant and Midshipman. You're right there with Lieutenant Commander Qin; he's our Chief Engineer."

Boxer set her duffel bag on her bunk and looked around. Lestor's bed was made, and a few personal items were on the built-in desk unit.

"Don't mind my stuff. If you need space, just let me know," Lestor said pleasantly.

Boxer opened her bag, pulled out her combat helmet, and set it on her side of the desk.

"That's all I keep out. You know, just in case," Boxer said, her dark eyes narrowing.

"I hope we won't have to deal with marauders on this voyage."

Boxer winked at her. "I live for it."

Lestor motioned to the wall closet. "Your clothes go there. Not much room, I'm afraid."

Boxer pulled out the rest of her gear, two duty uniforms, and fleet-issued undergarments. Lestor backed out of the room so that Layton could hear her.

"The officer's shower and latrine is down the hall to the left. The captain and FO have priority. After that, it's first come, first served."

Layton nodded and went back to unpacking in his cabin.

Boxer gave Lestor a wink and a suggestive smirk before she started stripping off her formal black uniform. Her body was lean and physically fit, the hard body of a warrior. Lestor turned to leave. "What's your first name, Lieutenant?" Boxer asked.

Lestor kept her eyes looking out the hatch. "Trin. Just so you know, I'm not attracted to females. We'll get along just fine if you stay out of my bed." She looked back at the now topless Boxer, who put up her hands in defeat. "Yes, ma'am. Can't blame a girl for trying."

Lestor shook her head and headed back to duty.

***

The *Weippe's* engine room was circular to accommodate the main stardrive. A series of tubes sprouted out of the spherical center of the magnetized target fusion drive, and pipes and banks of wires were scattered throughout the cramped room.

Standing at the instrument panel controlling the mains was a short man with spiked white hair that seemed to thin out on top of his broad head. His eyes were tiny slits most of the time, framed by deep wrinkles. Commander Qin was at the tail end of his long service career in the Fleet. He was a few years older than the Captain, and they had served together off and on for most of their thirty-year careers.

For the five enlisted ratings standing before him and the cooker, as he called the drive, he was an intimidating old man they were probably hoping would cut them some slack on their first voyage. He may look like someone's eccentric old grandfather, but he ran a tight ship and expected more from his young stokers than they usually expected of themselves.

"Petty Officer Cullers, I'm placing you in charge of these kids while I'm not on duty. If they screw up and damage my cooker, I'm gonna have your ass. Is that clear?"

Jacob Cullers quickly barked, "Aye, sir."

He was still only a few months out of NCO school and had yet to be in charge of anything more than his own butt. The other ratings looked even younger and more inexperienced than Cullers. There were two women, both of whom looked plain and simple-minded, the same as the two men. Good, maybe they will keep off each other for a while and focus on their jobs.

"I only have one rule for newbies: Don't break up my cooker. If you don't know what you're doing, seek help. This is a fine-tuned machine that will come apart very fast if you don't respect it. Do you understand?"

They all acknowledged in unison. Qin walked by, staring at them hard with his permanent squint. He stopped before a young kid with red hair and big baby-blue eyes.

"You ever been to space before, son?"

Qin's voice had lowered and now sounded like someone's grandfather.

"No, sir. This is my first assignment."

Qin pointed to the girl beside him. "Your first time, too?" She nodded and remembered to belt out, "Aye, sir."

Qin shook his head slowly and looked at the next boy. They were all too young for him to even consider them adults. "This isn't your first time aboard a starship, right?"

"No, sir."

This kid had rolled his sleeves up and was wearing a fluid scanner on his belt. His uniform was a white jumpsuit with patches from his last cruise. Qin could read *SS Sandervale* on the unit patch.

"Change out that patch and get one for the *Weippe*. Otherwise, ship-shape, son."

"Thank you, sir."

Qin hardly looked at the last woman. He could hear her exhale in relief as he returned to Petty Officer Cullers.

"Okay, people, here's the poop. As far as I know, this is just another escort cruise. If so, we have plenty of power to chase off pirates. Just do as you're told, and do it quickly, and we'll all get back to Allifax in one piece. I know the Captain well, and he'll probably not demand too much of us. Which is good because you're all wet behind the ears."

Qin momentarily eyed the gauges and readouts on the monitors and then looked back at his crew. They were young, depressingly so. But they looked like a decent bunch to him. There didn't seem to be a troublemaker among them. Time will tell whether that proved true or not. Some people never showed their true colors until they faced stressful situations. Considering the radiation and power contained in the fusion drive, they could either have a smooth voyage or become glowing bits of matter in less time than it took to realize something was wrong.

Chapter 3

Lieutenant Boxer relieved Lieutenant Lestor as Officer of the Day a few hours after boarding. Trin showed her how to check in the crew and ensured she knew her way around the decks enough to guide new people to their berths. Boxer hated being the OD, especially in port—a steady trickle of enlisted spacers arriving and departing as needed for tomorrow's launch.

When she took over, they were only half staffed, which meant she could expect at least another twenty arrivals, and who knew how many contractors still had to disembark. She passed the time making small talk with the enlisted rating, who seemed nice enough but was not on her defense team. She didn't care about his thoughts on life and the Fleet, but she pretended to sound interested, anyway.

About two hours into her shift, the Surface Army arrived: one major and several NCOs, all wearing combat fatigues and armed to the teeth. She had to ensure their plasma rifles were deactivated and their handguns were empty in accordance with weapons safety rules on a starship.

Major Bray was a muscular man in his late thirties with thick, spiked hair and beady gray eyes who seemed not to care about anyone who wasn't in the Surface Army.

"I didn't know we were expecting the army on this voyage. What's your mission, Major?" Boxer asked as professionally as she could.

"None of your business, Lieutenant," was Bray's curt reply.

Boxer handed him back his pistol, and he holstered it without taking an eye off of her. One of the NCOs was a tough-looking woman with hair as short as the men's. She had a distant look in her brown eyes that Boxer found irresistible. The trooper's name on the tape read Bryant, but she never returned Boxer's interest and said nothing.

After the soldiers left, Boxer called up the ship's payload manifest and immediately noticed more than the usual amount of small arms ammunition and something marked experimental. She cleared her screen, so the rating didn't notice what she had done and decided to do a bit of old-fashioned detective work.

"Starman, have you heard any odd scuttlebutt about this voyage?"

The kid scrunched up his face in a comical exaggeration of thinking. "Let me see. Nope. Nothing odd, ma'am."

"What about that new gun turret? Kinda big for a boat this size," Boxer prompted.

He nodded thoughtfully and piped up, "Oh yeah, the contractors that installed it mentioned that they thought it was for some kind of special mission. My bunkmate said he thought we were going pirate hunting with it, like some kind of search-and-kill mission. I told him he was full of it. Corvettes left that stuff to the Destroyers."

"Agreed."

Another couple of spacers entered the airlock, and her attention was diverted. But she continued to ponder what she had discovered. Surface Army troops traveled on all Fleet starships, but a Corvette usually warranted two enlisted soldiers. Having all NCOs and an O-3 in charge was highly unusual. That, coupled with the outsized railgun turret and various wild rumors, had her curiosity piqued. Maybe this was going to be an interesting cruise after all.

***

The *Weippe's* wardroom was just as small and crowded as the rest of the ship. It contained a rectangular table that seated six officers and was tended to by a single steward. The captain sat at the head of the table and was served first. To his immediate left sat Lieutenant Lestor, the ship's navigator; Lieutenant Torven, the scanning officer; and Major Bray from the Surface Army.

To the captain's immediate right was the first officer, Lieutenant Vance. Then there was Lieutenant Boxer, Chief of Security, and Commander Qin, Chief Engineer. Seats were dictated by tradition and the captain's leisure.

Lestor and Torven arrived first and lingered in the narrow room as the steward poured them a glass of their drink of preference, either concentrated juice or water. They wore their gray duty uniforms, identical in practical styling to their dress blacks. Each wore a single braid on his or her sleeve, denoting their rank. A gold specialty badge was pinned above their left breast pocket, and a name tag on their right. The Stellar Fleet uniforms were descended from a long line of military uniforms from many services and nations in the Federation's past. The resulting cut and fit flattered both sexes and was comfortable to wear over long duty hours.

Major Bray entered the room and was quickly followed by Lieutenant Boxer. She seemed to be tailing him, her dark eyes watching his every move. Bray moved to the far corner of the room and appeared unwilling to engage in small talk with the others.

"What's with the Army? Too good to be seen mingling with a bunch of Fleeters?" Lestor whispered to Boxer.

"I think he's on some kind of secret mission. Have you seen the ship's manifest?"

Lestor shook her head and took a drink of ice water.

"Let's just say we are more than armed enough to dissuade pirates from attacking our convoy."

Lestor raised an eyebrow and watched Commander Qin enter the room. He was the shortest of them and seemed to maneuver himself around the room with the ease and familiarity of someone who had been here for many years. He snatched a dinner roll off the table and started eating it dry, with no butter. Seeing the Surface Army uniform, Qin went up to introduce himself. "Major, nice of the Army to send such a distinguished officer on our cruise."

Bray regarded the petite man with apparent disdain. "Commander, he said. He didn't have time to say more before Lestor called the room to attention.

Captain Xander strolled in, waving for everyone to take their seats. The steward immediately poured the captain some wine.

"Where's Number One?" Xander asked, putting his napkin in his lap.

Lestor and Boxer traded shrugs. Xander was about to get annoyed when he noticed Qin waving with his bread.

"Qin, old buddy! Nice to have you along again," the Captain said with a smile.

"Pleasure's all mine, sir."

"I trust you have the cooker all ship-shape?"

"Indeed, I do, sir. Just give the word."

The captain looked around and then decided to start without his first officer.

"Okay, Davey, let's see what Cook has prepared for us."

The steward nodded and immediately brought the main course, a roast with all the trimmings. This would be their first and last good meal before launch. Once underway, the meals would become much less extravagant.

Lieutenant Vance entered the room and hastily took his seat beside Xander. "Please pardon my tardiness, Captain."

Xander regarded him with a knowing eye. "Are we all aboard and settled, Number One?"

Vance understood that his captain was referring to the crew. "Aye, sir. A few lost starmen and one contractor overstaying his welcome a bit."

"Happens every trip, doesn't it, Qin?" the Captain said, taking a bite of pork.

Qin nodded as he finished chewing. "Remember that poor kid who got locked out on his EVA when the ship launched? He turned up missing, and nobody could find him for hours."

Xander chuckled as everyone looked at Qin for a resolution to the story. The old man took a drink to draw out the tension, then finished. "Someone heard him banging on the ship with a wrench he had taken. The poor kid was damn near on his last breath when they hauled him in. He survived."

"That was my first Captain's Mast. Brought him and his supervisor up on desertion charges. I eventually dropped the charges, but it sure had the crew's attention for that cruise."

The conversation lulled as everyone enjoyed their dinner. Captain Xander finished before anyone else and immediately started reviewing his expectations of them. "I'm hands off for the most part, but the moment I see you flailing around, I'm going to take over, and you definitely won't like how I do things. I don't suffer fools lightly. I can't divulge much about our mission until we depart. But I can tell you that it won't be boring. Where we're going, there could be trouble. What kind of trouble we don't know, but Fleet saw fit to give us a bigger cap gun and more support from the Army. So don't get in their way," he looked over at Boxer, "and let them do their thing."

She glanced from the Captain to Major Bray, who flashed her a warning look before sipping his wine.

"Navigation," Xander said, changing the subject. "Set our initial course for Negram. We'll be making a series of jumps in a jigsaw manner to conceal our eventual destination."

Lieutenant Vance asked what everyone else was thinking. "Who are we trying to deceive, Captain?"

Xander glanced at Bray and said, "We don't know."

***

Early in the next shift, the bridge of the *Weippe* was hopping as the ship prepared to depart. Lieutenant Vance lingered near the captain's chair, not daring to take it for fear of the captain coming on deck and wanting it back. He kept checking his chronograph, wondering when the old man would show. They were ten minutes past the scheduled launch time, and everyone was beginning to get nervous. A Destroyer was scheduled to take its berth as soon as it was launched. Their FO had already contacted the *Weippe* to ask about a problem. Vance politely said no and cut the connection rather abruptly because he was nervous that he hadn't found any problems, and he was flat jealous of the Destroyer FO's position. He should be on a Destroyer, not this rusted old boat on the fringes of the known universe.

"Lieutenant, the *Terminus* is contacting us again for an update on our status," Sub-Lieutenant Lestor said from her station.

Vance waved her off.

"It's their captain, sir."

Vance returned to the captain's chair and opened the line. The Destroyer's captain appeared on the main screen. His aged face was taut with strain. He was in no mood to suffer delays.

"What's wrong, *Weippe*? My crew's been in space for six months. We'd like to get the hell out of this tin can."

Vance stood up straight and responded without hesitation. "It's taking us longer than expected to get the mains online, Captain. They had to crowbar the tunnel drive into this old nuclear hull, and I don't think it was a good fit. We'll be underway on retros if we have to."

The captain's face seemed to relax slightly as he shook his head. "Must be hell stuck on that old bucket, son."

Vance wanted to agree with the man, but that would look bad in front of the crew.

"Oh, we manage, sir. Have a better one."

Lestor terminated the connection. Vance looked at her, and she shrugged. "I didn't like his attitude."

Vance nodded and then started calling for all lines to be retracted. He was going to leave whether the captain was on deck or not. "Engineering, bridge. Give us everything you've got. We're busting out of here."

"Aye, sir, all systems full charge," said Petty Officer Cullers over the intercom.

As he took the captain's chair, Vance wondered why Qin had not replied. He was probably busy fixing something. He checked the secondary screens that showed the docks on both sides of the Corvette. "Helm, all ahead departure speed."

"All ahead, departure speed, aye."

The bridge hatch swung open at the back of the room, and Captain Xander padded in barefoot and wearing his old, worn service robe. His silver hair was messed up, and he yawned before saying anything.

"Number One, aren't we supposed to be at our first jump location? Why are we still in port?"

Vance started to say something and then thought better of it. "Yes, sir. Some minor issues delayed us. We are departing now."

Xander looked around through squinted eyes and then turned to leave. "I'll be down in the galley if you need me." He was gone before Vance could ask if he wanted to take the con.

***

The galley was about as clean as you could make a fifty-year-old room. The ship's cook, Petty Officer Seif Odem, had been to space with Captain Xander for the last five years. He knew just how the man liked his coffee, and he knew to expect him on launch day.

Xander entered the galley and sat at the stainless steel preparation table. Odem placed a mug of steaming brew before him and waited for the captain to consume it like a thirsty man in the desert guzzling water. Xander sat back with a content smile on his bearded face as his hands cupped the warm mug.

"Thanks, Seif, that's just what I needed."

Odem poured him a refill and dropped one cube of sugar and a tarnished silver spoon.

"I was wondering how long you would make them wait before you had your coffee, sir."

Xander stirred the coffee and said, "The *Terminus* is waiting for us to leave to dock. Their crew is probably ready to rebel if they don't dock soon. They've been in space for half a year."

Both men chuckled as Chief Qin came in from the stern passageway.

"What'd I miss?"

"I had Artie pester the new FO about getting underway. It was perfect," Xander said. His old blue eyes were becoming more alive with each sip of Java.

Qin snapped his fingers and laughed. "I wish I could have seen that one."

Qin smiled at the antics of his old friend. Odem set a fresh cup of green tea before the Chief.

"Remember the time the mains nearly melted down on launch day?" Qin asked as he scooped up his cup and sipped his tea.

Xander squinted a bit as he tried to recall the exact mission. "Wasn't that the one we escorted a bunch of cattle out to Ocherva?"

Qin nodded. "This poor rating was told to clean something. What was it? I can't remember. He goes into the blast chamber without telling anyone, and the ship launches. The damn fool was tossed about and zapped with God knows how much radiation."

Xander joined in, remembering the story now. "Didn't someone hear him clanging around?"

Odem was busy chopping vegetables for a stew at his preparation counter, but he listened with interest to the old spacer's story. Odem turned to face the table, his dark brows furrowed. "Did they get to him before, well, you know?"

Qin's eyes squinted nearly shut as he laughed. "Damn fool suffered radiation burns, but he survived."

Xander shook his head and scratched his gray beard. "Kid went on to be a decent starman, as I recall. I think he's on the *Sokol* now."

"They use him as a navigation beacon. He glows so brightly," Qin laughed.

The two men reminisced about old times before Xander got up to leave. He stretched while yawning and then handed Odem his mug. "Thanks, Seif; I'd better get changed and head to the bridge. We should be just about at the first jump point."

Xander looked down at Qin, who was still finishing up his tea. "You'd better make sure your kids haven't broken anything, Kang."

Qin nodded as he waved off the captain. The two men used the launch to test their crew's readiness. If the First Officer couldn't get the ship launched, or the Petty Officer in charge of Engineering couldn't get the mains spun up, both senior officers knew they would have their work cut out for them. It was a pretty smooth departure by their standards.

Chapter 4

Whe Captain Xander finally showed up on the bridge in uniform and ready for his shift, the *Weippe* was coming out of its first short jump. Vance exited the command seat and stood by as Xander sat down.

"Ready to come out of tunnel space, sir. Do we have the next heading?"

Xander looked around to see if everything was okay before responding. The bridge was fully staffed, and the ship seemed steady in tunnel space. He dipped his head and said, "Bring us out, Number One."

Vance turned to Sub-Lieutenant Lestor and nodded. She worked her controls, and the old Corvette started to rattle and shake as it fell into standard space—tunneling drives carved through space and time by creating short wormholes. A starship could travel for hours or days inside a tunnel and then pop into real space without expending much energy. The *Weippe* soon smoothed out, and the stars of the Outer Rim redshifted back to normal.

Qin's voice sputtered over the intercom. "Engine Room, all systems nominal. Ready for the next jump."

Xander pressed the mike button and replied, "Thanks, Chief, bridge out."

"Helm, reset the heading to the following coordinates," Xander said as he punched some numbers into the keypad on his armrest.

"Aye, Captain. Coordinates set," Lestor said.

Xander looked at Vance and stroked his beard. "Commence the jump."

Everyone on the bridge secured themselves with lap belts as the tiny ship's bow swung around to the new heading. After a few moments to let the navigation computers calculate their jump, the stars on the main viewer began to blue shift and then fade away into the blackness of tunnel space. The ship shuddered noticeably but not alarming.

Xander pressed the intercom mic again and said, "Senior staff to the wardroom ASAP." He turned to Chief Petty Officer Galen Hall. "Mr. Hall, you have the con. We won't be long."

Hall stood up from his post and saluted. "Aye, sir, I have the con."

Xander waved a hand in front of his face and led the officers off the bridge.

***

Lieutenant Vance was the last one into the wardroom, and he secured the hatch behind him. Everyone else was already seated at the table. Captain Xander waited for Vance to take his seat and began in a disarmingly gentle, soft tone.

"As you may have already noticed, our mission will not be to escort commerce ships. We are proceeding to the Al-Shatar system to answer a distress beacon from the *SS Wayfinder*. The captain of the *Wayfinder* set off an emergency beacon."

Lieutenant Lestor spoke up. "Wasn't the *Wayfinder* an exploration ship funded by the Gunnel Corporation?"

Xander slowly nodded, pleased that someone had been paying attention to the news. Exploration ships were sent out every so often by the big, multi-planet industrials to search for new resources they could exploit. There wasn't always much in the way of fanfare, but this mission was notable for having traveled the farthest outside of known space.

Xander opened a control panel at his end of the table and turned on the central holo-projector. A three-dimensional image of the *Wayfinder* spun slowly above the table. It was a long, spindly starship not unlike a Fleet Destroyer. It had tunnel drive engines but carried more body sections filled with supplies for an extended mission in deep space.

"From what we can tell, she was in orbit of a greenish world with a single ground team on the surface when she was hit," Xander motioned to Major Bray to take over the presentation.

Bray started in with a laser-sharp intensity that everyone in the room noticed. "Two smaller vessels did an initial pass on the civilian starship. There were no hostile moves other than the unusually close approach. When they circled back around for a second pass, they opened fire on the *Wayfinder* and presumably destroyed her."

He opened his control panel and changed the image to a flat screen that showed what appeared to be the ship's viewer footage from the bow of the *Wayfinder*. Two flat-winged craft with cylindrical fuselages opened fire with red energy beam weapons from their wingtips. After they fired, the image went to static and then switched off.

Xander cleared his throat to recapture everyone's attention. "Fleet has instructed us to search for survivors. We have Major Bray and his people along for added security. I have no orders to find possible hostiles, but I think it's pretty apparent that if they engage us, we are striking back as hard as possible."

Vance looked from the captain to the major as he asked, "Do we know who these aggressors are?"

Xander shook his head curtly, and Bray hunched his shoulders. "We don't know for sure. Speculation has it they are the elusive Blue-Devils."

Lestor laughed out loud. "You're kidding, right? Blue-Devils are bogeyman stories parents tell their children so they don't wander off on alien planets."

Boxer rolled her eyes and looked back at the Captain. "She's right, sir. We can't possibly take that seriously. Al-Shatar is unexplored. It's probably a sentient race from that area or nearby."

Qin started chuckling to himself. Captain Xander called him out. "What's so funny, Kang?"

"'Boo hoo, here comes the Blue, going to carve you up and tear you down. Blue-Devils come for you from the deep, dark black.' I used to tell my kids a horrible poem. My wife hated it because she blamed me for all their night terrors. But my kids never left our sides, either. So I guess it worked," Qin said.

Lestor raised her hand as if to say, "See, nonsense."

Then Qin pulled up his left sleeve to show off an impressive scar across the length of his forearm. Everyone stared at it as his voice dropped down several octaves. "Nobody was laughing on the *Hunley's* away team. Four of us went down to the surface, and only I returned."

He looked over at Bray with narrowed eyes. "You think you're ready for anything, Major. But you'll not be ready for them."

Xander wasn't sure if his old friend was pulling his leg. The room was so quiet you could hear the air circulation fans blowing. He knew Kang had that scar, but he had never heard how he had come to have it. Now he knew. The *SS Hunley* was a deep-space hauler that crashed on Arkab and had to wait months to be rescued. Qin was the sole survivor of that ship, and until this day, Xander had never heard him mention it.

"Okay, people, let's not lose any sleep over this. Lieutenant Boxer, please give the Major whatever he needs to help secure this ship. Number One, I need to develop an escape plan if we find ourselves over our heads. Whatever happens, do not go home the same way we came. Jig and jag across this area of space to throw off our scent. Fleet doesn't want a hostile alien invasion because we didn't cover our trail."

"Aye, sir."

"Also, let's arm up the senior staff. Lieutenant Boxer, can you see that we all get handguns?"

Boxer sat up and leaned toward the Captain. "Sir, we only have enough for a few officers."

Xander seemed surprised to hear that. "Really? Why?"

"Fleet policy is only to carry the minimum amount unless mission needs dictate more. Since we are only now learning what the mission will be..." her voice trailed off.

"Lieutenant, come see me on the hangar deck. I have enough pistols for every NCO and officer."

Boxer nodded politely to the Major and smiled thinly.

Xander stood up from the table, prompting everyone else to stand. "I don't anticipate any trouble. They are probably light-years away from there by now. But we may find survivors who need our help. I want everyone ready at action stations when we arrive. Dismissed."

***

After making several more tunnel jumps, edging closer to their target, Lieutenant Vance gathered his subs in the wardroom for a brief heart-to-heart. Boxer had armed them with appropriate weapons that she had obtained from Major Bray. They each had a large-caliber, Surface Army-issue handgun. Most of them had not completed range safety courses lately or even qualified on their weapons, so Boxer did an impromptu safety refresher in the shuttle bay as each crew member came off duty.

Vance was reasonably confident in his ability to handle a pistol, but he wanted to ensure his staff would be ready to use their weapons if and when they were called upon. They were all military members and had accepted commissions that promised they would defend the Federation from all enemies, foreign or domestic. But Vance wanted to know if they had any second thoughts about pulling the trigger.

"I just wanted to ensure we were all on the same page before we made the final jump to Al-Shatar. You've each been issued a weapon, and Lieutenant Boxer assures me you are qualified to carry and use it. What I want to know is if anyone has any second thoughts about killing?" Vance asked.

He looked at Lestor, who grimly nodded back to him. Then he looked at Torvin, who pushed his glasses back onto his nose and said with a cough, "Yeah, sure. But I'd rather not."

Boxer and Vance exchanged sharp looks. "If something were attacking you or anyone on this ship, you would not hesitate to kill it, right?" Boxer asked.

Torvin rolled his eyes and looked down. "I, I would like to think that's what I'd do. But in all honesty, I'm not sure what I would do."

Lestor touched Torvin's arm with her hand. "Look, I don't think any of us wants to kill anyone."

Torvin looked up at Vance. "I'm pretty sure that if my life were in danger, I'd pull the trigger."

That was all Vance cared about. The chances of a Scanning Officer defending himself on the bridge were pretty low, but he wanted assurance that the kid would fire if provoked. He had no idea what they would be facing and needed to be able to count on his staff if the shit hit the fan.

Boxer patted the butt of her pistol with the palm of her hand and winked at him. "I won't hesitate, sir."

Vance cracked a smile for the first time that day.

***

Lieutenant Boxer assembled her security team and took them to the shuttle bay. She wanted to make sure they were on the same page regarding boarding tactics and fields of fire on a confined vessel. They were all dressed in the same utility uniform that the army wore. The fabric was coated in adaptive camouflage that blended with whatever color was predominant in the area. Aboard a ship, their uniforms wore a gray and black patchy pattern.

Boxer opened the hatch and stepped inside the cold hangar bay. Major Bray and his troops were on the far side, cleaning their weapons. Gun barrels, disassembled firing mechanisms, and oily rags were everywhere. Boxer looked back at her ratings and frowned. They were not the lean, mean killing machines that Bray commanded. They were just four kids from various parts of the ship whose job it was to leave their post and defend the ship when needed.

"Stay here," she said to them.

She walked as nonchalantly as possible over to Major Bray and, when he noticed her, snapped him a crisp salute.

"Major, do you mind if I review some things with my folks? We'll stay on this side of the bay."

Bray shook his head but said nothing. He was in the process of cleaning the barrel of his rifle and didn't look as if he gave a rat's ass what she and her people did.

Boxer noticed that some of the soldiers' weapons didn't look like standard army-issue rifles—they didn't even look like projectile weapons. She guessed that one was a small squad automatic railgun, but the other one was clearly some sort of laser rifle.

"What interesting toys you have, sir. Mind if I take a closer look?"

Bray suddenly stood up. "Yes."

Boxer backed away with a sheepish grin and saluted him again. This time, he didn't return the salute; he just watched her head back to the other side of the hangar.

When she returned to her ratings, she had them form up in boarding defensive positions and practice moving and covering each other. A silent ballet of gun pointing and feet shuffling ensued. They were doing the best they could, but they lacked symmetry and cohesion. It would be challenging to accomplish that with unmotivated kids fulfilling an extra detail. Boxer looked back across the bay and noticed the female member of the Army squad. She had dirty blonde hair and fair white skin. Her face was devoid of emotion. Boxer felt an inexplicable pull to her, even though she had never met her and didn't even know her name.

Fraternization with the non-commissioned officers was frowned upon but not forbidden on a starship. Command understood shipboard life's limited social situation and allowed some leeway in space. It was tolerated as long as the two individuals were not in the same chain of command. Boxer stopped watching the woman cleaning her weapons and reluctantly focused on her charges.

Chapter 5

Sub-Lieutenant Lestor was deep into her late shift on the bridge when telemetry from the Al-Shatar system started trickling in. Lieutenant Torven was on duty at the scanner station. His ever-present soundproof headphones were on, and his fingers darted over his touchscreen as he worked.

"What have you got, Layton?" Lestor asked after touching his shoulder to get his attention. She had left the captain's chair and stood over Torven, looking down at the flickering data on his screens.

"Trinary star system, only two of them snuggled up close to each other. I'm reading about thirty planetary bodies and at least three asteroid belts, one of which I think goes around both stars. Hard to tell for sure at this distance."

Boxer called up the flight plans for the *SS Wayfarer* and had them overlaid onto the newly created star system map on the main display. It looked like they were supposed to go to the fourth planetary system in what Torven had labeled Al-Shatar Beta, the smaller of the two close-in stars.

"Lots of stellar radiation in the system," Torven said.

Lestor moved her hand over the armrest of the captain's chair, and the image zoomed in on the fourth planet. It was still just a fuzzy green ball, but she could see there was plenty of proto-planetary nebula in the system. In fact, this organic matter was causing the greenish color.

"It would appear to be a strange area to look for life or at least a planet capable of harboring life." Lestor watched the screen update with clearer images every few minutes. It occurred to her after a time that they might be seeing things no human had ever witnessed before. At least no one who was alive now.

"Do you pick up any tunnel signatures or hulls in the area? We don't even know if their ship was destroyed or damaged."

Torven shook his head. "Can't get a good scan now, but I'm ready to hit it when we come out of tunnel space."

Lestor glanced at the mission clock and noted that it was about time for the first shift to come on duty. She stood up and started walking around the tiny bridge, making sure it looked presentable.

"Shift change is coming up, people; look sharp. Torven, you're probably pulling a double. I imagine the Captain wants you on until we find some sign of the *Wayfarer*."

Torven shook his head and said, "Not a problem. This is history we're making. No Fleet ship has ever been to this system."

The bridge hatch cracked open, and Lieutenant Vance stepped inside. He was wearing duty grays with every crease sharp enough to cut paper. Lestor came to attention, ready to be relieved of her lead position. She would also pull a second shift until Vance or the Captain relieved her. She watched Vance approach, his eyes mainly on the main viewer. When he was in front of her, she saluted.

"Lieutenant Lestor, by your command, sir."

Vance waved a smart salute. "Do we have a decent map of the system yet, Lieutenant?"

Lestor turned to the main viewer. "Data is streaming in as fast as we can probe, sir. I have the main viewer updating live images and telemetry."

"That's not what I asked. Can we navigate with what we have now?"

Lestor's brow furrowed. *Why did he have to be such an ass?*

"Yes, sir. We have more than enough to achieve orbital velocities around all the planetary-sized objects."

Vance tilted his head and said, "Excellent. Take the helm then."

Lestor moved to her station and logged in, resisting the urge to bore holes into the back of Vance's head with her eyes. She watched Vance move to the captain's chair and sit down as if it were his own. He fiddled with the armrest controls and soon entered coordinates after the jump.

"I have the con. Prepare to exit tunnel speed. Engineering, are we ready to exit?"

There was a short pause before Petty Officer Cullers responded. "Aye, sir. Give the word."

Vance clicked the intercom. "Standby."

"Helm, after we exit, set course for the fourth planet, coordinates incoming."

Lestor saw the numbers on her screen and quickly set a course: "Course set and locked in."

Vance glanced around the room and then up at the clock. It was ten seconds before the shift change. Several enlisted ratings entered the bridge and went to their duty stations. Vance stood up and moved to his customary position. He waited at attention for the Captain to show. Lestor kept an eye on him as she reconfirmed her course. He sure was a by-the-book individual, she thought.

The ship's PA sputtered on and the Captain's voice spoke, "Senior staff to the wardroom for a status briefing. Captain out."

Lestor watched as Vance eased his posture and looked around, slightly confused. Clearly, he didn't know what to make of the Captain's unorthodox ways. Captains always did their briefings on the bridge at shift change. Vance scrambled to anoint someone in charge while Lestor and Torven took their leave.

***

Everyone had found his or her seat by the time Vance got to the wardroom. The Captain was sipping his coffee, and the other officers were organizing their reports on datapads. Vance took his seat with a polite nod to the captain.

"Good morning, Lieutenant. Why don't you start us off? Any concerns about the readiness of the ship?" Xander asked, taking a sip.

Vance flashed Qin a quick look before he spoke. The old man didn't seem concerned in the slightest. "Sir, I'd like to increase engine efficiency to ninety percent. The best we seem to be able to muster per tunnel jump is around seventy percent."

Xander saw Qin's face begin to redden and put up a hand to stop him from saying anything rash. "Number One, this ship is probably older than your father. Maintaining a seventy percent efficiency during tunnel jumps is more than acceptable. You won't get any better from this old girl."

Vance shook his head. "I respectfully disagree, sir."

Qin started to wind up, his blood pressure no doubt spiking. "Impossible!"

Vance looked to Qin and maintained his self-assurance: "Commander, the stardrive is not as old as the hull. It's the latest design, albeit a few years behind the newest in the fleet. My point is, it can and should be functioning better. There are new stabilization techniques in use throughout the fleet. My last assignment was on the *Greinke*, which has the same drive. We routinely achieved ninety percent jump efficiency."

Qin slammed his hand down on the metal table, causing some people to jump. "That's because the *Greinke* has a completely different containment field. And do you know where she is right now? In dry dock for a complete drive overhaul as a result."

Xander slowly looked back at his first officer. Vance lowered his eyes and quickly looked up something on his datapad to verify Qin's words. The Captain and everyone else waited patiently. Qin shook his head and mumbled something only he understood.

Vance looked up with egg on his face. "I apologize, Commander. You are correct."

Xander and Qin exchanged grins. "Mr. Vance, I appreciate you taking the time to confirm what the Chief Engineer said, but from now on, I expect you to believe whatever the man tells you. Understand?"

Vance nodded and mumbled weakly, "Aye, sir."

Xander moved on while his first officer stewed quietly to himself. "Layton, what have you got on the Al-Shatar system?"

Layton Torven sat up and spoke in a cracking voice that quickly evened out. "It's a trinary system with the third star orbiting far enough to encircle the other two—a total of sixteen planetary bodies and multiple asteroid belts. There are patches of leftover stellar matter between the stars that haven't gelled into anything. Most of the system is bathed in heavy radiation. Gaseous planets are hot, and the rocky ones are barren of life. It's a young system, sir."

Xander nodded absently as Torven spoke, taking in the information. Then he turned his attention to Lestor. "Trin, do you anticipate any navigational problems due to this cosmic radiation?"

Lestor thought it through carefully before she answered. "No, sir. However, I believe some of our more refined scans will be affected, correct, Lieutenant?" she said to Torvin.

"Aye. We won't be able to track anything near the nebula, much less inside it. But it's not thick. We should be able to switch to optics and see into it."

Xander sat back and looked up at the pipes and wire bundles running along the ceiling. "Layton, see what you can do to find any remains of the *Wayfarer*. Get creative. We don't want to linger out here longer than we must."

"Aye, sir."

"Number One, keep the wide scans on active search as soon as we arrive in the system, and don't turn them off until we leave. I don't want to get caught with my pants down."

"Aye, sir."

"Major Bray, are your people ready for action?" Xander asked the stoic soldier at the far end of the table.

"Yes, sir. All our systems are checked out, and my people are ready for anything." His voice had the ring of self-confidence that always seemed to come from professional soldiers.

"Let's hope they are not needed," Xander said.

***

Late into the shift, the Captain had retired for the night, and Vance had sent Torven and two bridge ratings back to their quarters. They would be coming out of tunnel space early in the first shift, and he wanted everyone to be alert and ready for possible action stations. Lieutenant Lestor was sitting at the scanner station normally occupied by Torven, idly watching the incoming data from the long-range scanners. Her eyes were heavy, and she propped her head up with one hand as data scrolled by on her screens.

Vance came over behind her, and she sat up with a yawn. "I don't think Al-Shatar is shaping up to be a very good place for humans," she said.

He looked at the scans and then back to her dark eyes, slack with sleep. "There must've been some reason they picked this system to explore. I mean, the companies don't like to waste money looking this far out for no return on their investment."

"I agree. But for the life of me, I don't see any value here. It's all very radioactive and devoid of any scarce resources."

Vance glanced back at the screens. "Do you think those green ships on the buoy cams were from around here?"

She sighed. "No, I don't. Nothing organic could survive long in this system."

Vance studied her face. She had high cheekbones and a strong jawline and was pretty enough to be in fashion or perhaps an actress. Her short, dark brown hair was cropped pixie-style. Most servicewomen had long hair and tied it into a single tail, just like the men. He wondered why she preferred a shorter style.

She noticed his stare and moved back from him a bit. "What?"

"Nothing. I just," he smiled. "I don't think they were from this system either. If I had to guess, they were advanced military scouts. But that's well beyond my pay grade."

Lestor refocused on her screens, and Vance moved away. He circled the captain's chair and then sat down gently on it as if he were trying it out. His head looked up at the primary monitor. It was scrolling data from the scanners. *I was so close to a command of my own before being sent to this old scow.* He looked around at the worn-down bridge with a frown.

"You don't like the *Weippe* much, do you, sir?"

Vance turned around in the chair to face Lestor. "Does it show?"

She grinned. "It's not so bad. Sometimes, it's not the age but the experience that makes a ship."

Vance shook his head and held his thumb and forefinger close together. "I was this close to getting my own command."

"What happened? Did you piss someone off?"

"Not that I'm aware of. I have no idea what I did to deserve this." He glanced around again at the old, paint-chipped metal walls of the *Weippe* and sighed.

Lestor shrugged. "It's no use lamenting about it now. You're here, and we need you more than some fancy Destroyer does."

He could see the sincerity in her eyes. He nodded confidently and turned back around. Switching the view to focus on the shining green orb where the *Wayfinder* met her doom. If he had been assigned to a Destroyer, he wouldn't be here, where no fleet starship had ever been. Maybe she's right. Maybe this was where he should be.

Chapter 6

The *Weippe* entered real space near the final coordinates of the *Wayfinder*. Captain Xander had the crew at action stations. There was a noticeable increase in the level of tension on the bridge. Fully staffed with personnel, lights dimmed red, and the portholes covered, they were ready for anything.

Lieutenant Vance stood behind Torven's scanning station. "Nothing on the wide field scans, Captain."

Xander sat back in his chair, his leg crossed over and toe-tapping the air. He exuded confidence and calm as he watched the main screen. The space around the planet was bathed in a green and yellow nebula. It was otherworldly and eerie to a crew more accustomed to the black emptiness of space.

"Helm put us in a high orbit of ALS-429. Concentrate close-range scans on orbital debris and the surface," Xander said, his voice barely above a whisper.

"Orbital burn complete," Lestor said.

Vance approached the short-field scanner's station and suggested something to the Petty Officer seated there. A moment later, they got images. "Surface contacts," Vance said.

Xander punched a button on his armrest, transferring the scans to the main viewer. Nearly everyone looked up at them. They showed what looked like a standard shuttle lander near a ravine.

"Major Bray, prepare a ground team," Xander said into the ship's intercom.

"Roger that, Captain."

Xander looked over at Vance, who stood up straight. "Number One, go with him. See if you can locate any survivors. If not, try to ascertain what happened to them."

Vance saluted. "Aye, sir." He looked over to Lestor and motioned for her to join him.

Lieutenant Boxer pulled open the hatch to the bridge and rushed inside. "Captain, I'd like to go with the ground team."

Xander looked at her briefly and shook his head. "Negative. I need you on board in case we are attacked."

Boxer flinched at the rebuff, but she took her spot at the security station and started double-checking the main gun's readiness.

Lestor followed Vance off the bridge, securing the hatch behind her.

***

Lieutenant Lestor took the pilot's seat and strapped in inside the cramped shuttle. The crew chief had already started the twin ion thrusters, and the multifunction displays showed the status of her flight gauges. She eyed the virtual gauges as she adjusted her harness. They were all wearing pressure suits due to the toxic alien atmosphere they would be encountering.

Lieutenant Vance entered through the stern ramp and took the copilot seat. He hadn't flown a shuttle in months, but fortunately, Lestor was doing the flying. All he had to do was be ready in case of an emergency or if they were attacked. The shuttle had a small top turret that housed a one-centimeter rail gun. It was his job to fire it if they were attacked.

Major Bray and two troops entered last, taking the jump seats against the port and starboard walls. It was a bit jarring to look at them in their armored spacesuits with loaded rifles. Vance was glad they were on the same side. The soldiers secured a rectangular box to the floor between them. Vance looked back at them as they strapped in and gave him a thumbs-up. The stern hatch closed with a sucking sound, and he turned around to see the hangar bay door roll up and out of the way.

"Control, *Ericson*. Ready to launch," Lestor said.

Vance busied himself, checking the turret's readiness until finally, Control responded, "Copy *Ericson*, clear to launch."

Lestor wasted no time, and they immediately sped out of the bay and into the black. The tiny shuttle was rectangular, with a snub nose and stern. Two cylindrical engine pods hung off the sides and ran the length of the shuttle. As they cleared the *Weippe,* a strangely greenish world appeared below them. Vance caught himself gawking at the stark beauty of the shimmering globe.

It took about twenty minutes to descend through the planet's thin atmosphere the mapping software had named ALS-429. If it were up to him, he would have named it Jade because he'd never seen so many shades of green. The terrain looked like a surreal expressionist painting as they approached the landing site. Outside, the temperature was savagely cold, and the air was far too thin and toxic to breathe. He began agreeing with Lestor's assessment that this system was not ideal for human life.

"Sub-Lieutenant Lestor, please set us down a few meters from the *Wayfinder's* shuttle," said Major Bray.

"Aye, sir."

Lestor flared out well short of the other shuttle. As soon as their landing struts found purchase in the sandy soil, the back hatch was open, and the soldiers rushed out, weapons drawn. Vance unstrapped and grabbed a rifle on his way out.

***

Vance had been to several planets in his career, but nothing as stark and deadly as ALS-429. It was brighter than he would have thought with the light of two suns and the reflected light from a nearby gas giant. His face shield compensated by polarizing, but he still squinted from the glare. The ground was covered in a substrate that resembled green crystalline sand.

The soldiers surrounded and entered the *Wayfinder's* lander while Major Bray and Vance waited outside. Vance shouldered his rifle, not sensing any danger, and started to walk away, following footsteps in the dirt.

"Lieutenant, don't wander off," Bray cautioned.

Vance stopped and tried to get a reading with a handheld scanner he took from his belt. The scanner's screen was filled with static from the radiation. He noted the levels on the helmet HUD. They could be outside briefly before the radiation reached harmful levels.

"Bryant, check inside the lander," Bray ordered.

One of the soldiers, the woman, crawled into the lander and was out of sight for a few minutes. Vance was just beginning to get concerned when she came out, breathing heavily into her mic. "No survivors, sir. One body, female."

"What happened to her?" Bray asked.

"Looks like a sharp, bladed instrument hacked her up. It wasn't pretty in there."

Bray motioned for them to spread out. "Alright, people. Fan out and stay ready."

They all instinctively followed the multiple footprints that led over a nearby ridge. Vance looked back at the lander and tried to imagine what it would have been like to have been hacked to death. That's when he noticed the bloodstains on the windows of the lander. He turned away and swallowed hard. Bray had taken up the trailing position to cover their six, and Vance bumbled behind the female soldier.

When they got over the shallow ledge, Vance could see two bodies lying near what looked like a crash site of some kind. The soldiers moved in to secure the area and, after a few minutes, waved over him and Bray.

"That one's suit was breached, and he's dead. This one is alive but unconscious," the NCO reported.

Vance went down on his knee to look at the one still alive. He had never seen a spacesuit like it before. It was black, with tubes running to each limb like an ancient flight suit. Strange glyphs from a language he could not read were on the suit. The man's face mask was mirrored, and Vance couldn't get a good look inside. He could find no obvious signs of a fight and wondered if he had run out of supplies.

"Let's get him back to the ship," Bray ordered.

The two soldiers lifted the unconscious man and carried him back up the ravine. Bray and Vance examined the wreckage. It was mainly burned and in hundreds of shredded pieces, but judging from the overall shape, it could have been one of the green ships the *Wayfinder's* cameras recorded.

Bray started digging around inside what was probably the cockpit and pulled out a short, curved sword. He hoisted it up onto his shoulder and continued to search the area. Vance went to the dead man and rolled him over. He had several deep slashes across his chest. The blood had boiled away in the heat, and the skin around the wounds was still sizzling.

Bray had slid the sword into his backpack straps and touched Vance on his shoulder as he passed. "C'mon, Lieutenant. We're going to need to get this debris into the shuttle for further examination."

Vance stood up to follow the major. "But the shuttle won't be able to lift with much more weight."

"Then I'll stay behind."

Vance didn't like that but somehow knew the man would say it. When they reached the top of the ravine, Bray handed Vance the sword. "Take this back with the body. I'll maintain contact on an open channel. Hurry back."

He didn't give Vance a chance to respond before scrambling back down the ravine. Vance carried the blade over his shoulder like a rifle back to the shuttle. The soldiers had finished loading the body and were heading back.

"The Major's staying behind. We're taking back the body and returning," Vance told the higher-ranking male. His name tape read Rizzo.

"I can't leave him by himself. Breaks the battle buddy rule."

"Look, the radiation down here is too great. It's dangerous to leave one behind, much less two," Vance said.

Rizzo started walking back to the crash site. "Don't worry, these suits can take it. We'll see you back here ASAP, sir."

Vance didn't watch him leave. He turned around and headed back to the shuttle. After securing the rear hatch, Lestor started her ascent. They remained inside their suits until safely back inside the *Weippe*. Vance was about to remove his helmet when the female soldier stopped him. "We have to be decontaminated first. Help me get him into the airlock."

Vance did as the sergeant requested, and all three went into the nearest airlock together. A crewman from the *Weippe* cycled through the airlock and ran the decontamination sequence. After a few minutes, the hatch popped open, and crewmen helped load the survivor onto a stretcher and carried him to the tiny sickbay not far from the galley.

"You two get back down to the planet. Major Bray wants to remove some of that wreckage. Remind him that we need the bodies inside the lander, too, for ID and proper burial."

Sergeant Bryant saluted and followed Lestor back to the shuttle bay. Vance got out of his spacesuit and then headed to the sickbay to check on the survivor.

***

The sickbay was nothing more than a closet where injured personnel could undergo treatment. On a ship, the size of the *Weippe*, which was home to just under fifty people, sickbay was almost an afterthought. In fact, the ship didn't have one in the original hull design. Only after the twenty-five-year refit, when she was given a tunnel drive, did the shipbuilders carve a niche for sickbay. A simple containment pod with limited surgical abilities and no full-time medical officer was still better than nothing. The room was bigger than the pod and was jam-packed with containers from the galley. Storage space was at a premium on board, and the captain often authorized the cook to use the space for more food.

Two crewmen had laid the man out on the containment pod and were trying to figure out how to remove his helmet without injuring him. Lieutenant Torven, the volunteer medical officer, had never seen a suit like the man's. He attempted to remove the neck fastener when Lieutenant Boxer came in with her sidearm out and ready.

Torven looked up at her incredulously. "Really? The man's unconscious."

Boxer flexed her fingers around the handgun's trigger guard and reluctantly pointed it up. Torven dismissed the enlisted helpers and refocused on the latch, twisting and pulling in the same direction seemed to open it. There was a slight hiss as air from his suit escaped into the stillness of the sickbay.

The first officer stood at the tiny hatch and edged past Boxer. "Are you recording this?"

"No, should I?" Torven asked, his voice dripping with annoyance.

Vance grabbed a camera out of a nearby drawer and activated it. It hovered over their shoulders, out of the way, as it recorded the helmet removal. Torven carefully slid the helmet over the man's head and backed away when they saw his face. Boxer moved in closer, ensuring her pistol was armed. Vance backed up against the wall before stopping.

The man was not exactly human. He had the features of a human: two eyes, a nose, a mouth, and even ears, where a human had them. What made him different was his coloration and the brutish heavy brow line. His chin was less pronounced than a human's, and his nose was more expansive and flatter. He had jet-black hair and a goatee around his mouth.

"It's a damn caveman," Vance said.

"A blue one at that," Torven added. He reached behind his back and activated the medical scanner, which bathed the alien in blue light as it scanned from head to toe. Readings started scrolling by on nearby monitors. Torven watched them and then looked back at the unconscious man on the table.

"He's damn near human. Probably ninety-eight percent or so."

Boxer flexed her fingers on the handle of her pistol as she got a bit closer. "Maybe he's some kind of genetic experiment of the explorers."

Vance and Torven both looked at each other. Torven shook his head. "No, we don't screw with enhancing DNA anymore. At least not legally."

"Then what the hell is he?" Torven asked.

Torven moved closer to look at the man's pale blue face. Vance could tell his scanning officer was fascinated by his subject. "I can wake him up, and we can ask him," Torven said.

Vance shook his head no. "All the other bodies on the planet were dead humans. This must be one of the beings that attacked them."

The ship's speaker sputtered loudly, causing everyone but the blue man to jump. "Bridge to sickbay, report, Number One."

Vance moved to the wall-mounted speaker and pressed the transmit switch. "Vance here, Captain. I think you should come see this."

"On my way," the Captain's scratchy voice replied.

A few minutes later, Captain Xander entered the tiny room. They had removed the blue man's outer suit, and he was wearing a woven liner that shimmered red under the bright medical light.

"Who is he?" Xander asked.

"We think he's one of the attackers. He's not quite human, sir," Vance said. He felt as if he were merely stating the obvious.

Xander stared in awe at the alien. "He looks like one of Qin's Blue-Devils."

Chapter 7

By the third time touching down on the alien planet, Lieutenant Lestor began feeling like a garbage collector. When the rear boarding ramp lowered, only a few smaller bits of metal were tossed in the back. The next time she looked back, she saw the soldiers carefully placing the first of four black body bags. Even knowing the people inside were long dead, she still couldn't help but feel sorry for them. They had died horribly on a moon that could have easily killed them in a number of ways. They were probably the first people ever to have landed on the planet. They would all be remembered as the first people to die in the most distant world ever explored.

Major Bray and Sergeant Rizzo placed the final body bag against the shuttle's wall and then strapped it down for the return flight to the *Weippe*. The Captain had requested that the bodies be recovered so that they could be examined and given a proper burial in space. There was no room to keep them inside the ship, as space was already at a premium. Major Bray signaled their readiness and strapped himself in beside Lestor.

"Take us home, Sub-Lieutenant."

"Aye, sir."

It was a quiet ride back to the ship, where she watched the *Weippe* crewmen remove the bodies with as much care and reverence as possible. Lestor returned to her cabin afterward to change into her duty uniform. She was just sliding on her boots when the alarm sounded, followed by the mechanical sound of the ship's alert voice: "Attention the ship, attention the ship. Staff officers to the wardroom."

She gave herself a cursory look over in the mirror and headed out for the wardroom. Her newly issued service pistol lay forgotten on her bunk.

***

The wardroom was abuzz with chatter when Lestor entered right before Boxer. Boxer cornered her uncomfortably close. She had a serious look in her brown eyes. "Forget something, Sub-Lieutenant?" Boxer asked.

Lestor looked down as Boxer shoved the weapon into her hand and stepped away as if nothing had happened. Lestor affixed the gun to her belt and casually took her seat at the table. Boxer prowled around the small room to her seat across the table. Everyone stood up when the Captain entered with Vance at his side. Xander didn't sit down, determined to make this more of a stand-up meeting.

"Report, Major."

Xander looked to Major Bray, and the soldier cleared his throat before speaking. "We recovered four bodies from the planet. They had all been hacked to death with some sort of bladed weapon. Later, we found a short sword near a body at a nearby crash site."

Vance had been carrying the weapon and handed it to the Captain. Xander took it from his first officer and gently held it up to examine it. Vance knew that the

Captain was fond of ancient military history, and the sword looked like it could have come from a museum.

"A falchion of some kind," he said more to himself than anyone else.

"We found that in some wreckage near the blue-skinned man. He was unconscious but alive. It's not clear if his suit experienced a malfunction or if he was injured," Bray finished.

The Captain continued to examine the sword, lost in thought. Vance took the initiative to continue the briefing.

"We don't know if this is one of the aliens who attacked the *Wayfarer*, but that's our assumption now. The alien is restrained in sickbay, undergoing medical study by Lieutenant Torven."

Boxer pointed to the sword. "It seems hard to believe that a spacefaring species would use primitive-bladed weapons."

Vance agreed with that assessment as he waited for Bray to say something. The Major seemed unusually annoyed with those around him, or maybe it was the situation in general.

"Many warrior cultures hold on to primitive weapons as ritual tokens of their past. If this alien is from such a culture, we may not be equipped to counter them should they return," Bray said.

Vance saw the Captain refocus on the Major. He set down the sword carefully on the table before him. "Show us the prisoner."

Major Bray activated the central holoprojector, and a life-size recording of the blue man appeared before them. Qin gasped and stepped back from the table.

"It's one of them, a Blue-Devil," Qin said.

"Are you sure, old friend?" Xander asked.

Qin nodded emphatically. "I suggest you kill him now, Major. Before he..."

An attention alarm cut him off, and an automated voice reverberated throughout the ship. "Attention, the ship. Attention, the ship. Intruder alert, deck two, engineering." Major Bray was through the hatch with Boxer on his heels before the message finished.

The alarm was still sounding when the room speaker buzzed for attention. Vance answered. "Vance here."

"Sir, this is Cook. Lieutenant Torven is dead, and that Blue-Devil has escaped."

The room cleared as everyone scrambled to get to battle stations. Captain Xander stayed behind, picking up the falchion and holding it admiringly.

***

Sergeant Rizzo joined Major Bray in the corridor, and Rizzo handed him a rifle. Boxer drew her handgun and shouted into her communicator for her security team to meet her in Engineering. As she blew past the Galley, she saw a crowd around the sickbay and stopped. "Belay that. Meet me in Sickbay."

Boxer pushed her way through the enlisted ranks, jockeying for a view. "Make a hole, people. Make a hole."

When she got to the entrance hatch, she saw the pool of blood and the lifeless body of Lieutenant Torven.

"Looks like the prisoner gutted him and bolted. People saw him heading in the direction of Engineering," Odem said. He was opening a sheet to lay over the body.

Boxer had never seen a dead body before. Certainly not as graphically killed as poor Torven. She stepped back away from the sight and refocused on finding the alien. Two of her security troops showed up, weapons drawn.

"Follow me. He's heading to Engineering."

She pushed back more onlookers and hurried down the long, narrow corridor traversing the ship's center. Engineering was in the stern section, and the only way to it was through a narrow tube big enough to walk through.

When they reached the transfer tube, Boxer stopped and told her men to stay put and not let the alien back into the ship's main body. Their startled faces nodded, and they muttered, "Yes, ma'am."

She stepped into the dimly lit tube by herself. The pathway was clear, so she picked up her pace and double-timed it to the end of the tube. It angled into an antechamber that surrounded the Engineering. Several ratings in white jumpsuits ran past her, trying to get as far away as possible.

Boxer slid the safety off her pistol and held it firmly ahead of her in both hands. Before she could get into Engineering, she heard several shots from large-caliber rifles. *Dammit, they can't fire near the reactor,* she said to herself.

Petty Officer Cullers walked out suddenly with his hands raised slightly.

"Did they get the alien?" Boxer asked. Cullers looked past her and spoke to Qin, who had just arrived, panting.

"Sir, they cornered him near the intercooler. No alarms sounded, but we'll need to check it over."

Qin's narrow eyes were wide as he motioned for Cullers to get behind him. Boxer raised her pistol again and walked into the main Engineering room. It was the second-largest room aboard the *Weippe* after the shuttle bay, but you wouldn't know it by looking around. The

Magnetized Target Fusion drive was like a giant piston engine with a central sphere containing a rotating molten lead-lithium core. Compressed plasma was forced into fusion inside the engine.

Boxer saw some dark figures on the other side of the drive and cautiously approached. As she got closer, she began to hear voices.

"Keep your boot on his throat. I got his hands," Rizzo said.

"Bastard's not going anywhere, Sarge," Bryant boasted.

As Boxer approached the drive, Major Bray held his rifle on the subdued alien. He motioned for her to stand back. Then he said, "Lieutenant, clear the way. We're taking him to the airlock."

Boxer didn't question the move and immediately backed out of the room. Outside Engineering, she ordered Qin and Cullers back into the ship's main body. As she was herding them out, the soldiers dragged the still thrashing and grunting alien along behind her. His hands were tied behind his back, and his legs were bound with similar plastic bands. It took Rizzo, no slouch of a man, pulling in concert with Bryant to drag the prisoner down the metal floor.

As she went, Boxer cleared back the curious crew, ensuring the soldiers had the space to get the prisoner to the starboard airlock. Once they tossed him inside, they backed out and shut the heavy metal hatch. Major Bray watched the still struggling alien inside, writhing in fury in the cold metal room.

"That should hold him," Boxer said. There were no controls inside the airlock for coming aboard. You had to rely on someone inside to let you in. This was primarily a defensive move on the designer's part. Space pirates were a big concern when it came to boarding parties, and airlocks were their favorite targets. Of course, it was just as easy to blow a hole in the ship and come in, but even ruthless pirates would rather not destroy a ship they could later use.

"Gonna space your ass, pal," Bray mumbled.

Boxer and Rizzo exchanged looks. She could tell he had issues with that. His eyes betrayed his compassion despite his job. Bryant seemed indifferent. She rolled her brown eyes and looked away.

"Bridge, this is Major Bray. The prisoner is contained in the starboard airlock. Permission to space him."

"Permission denied. Get up here, Major."

Bray swore a blue streak and stormed off towards the bridge. Boxer tipped her head to Rizzo, who assured her with a confident nod that he wouldn't kill the alien. He and Bryant took up positions in front of the airlock.

***

Vance had taken Torven's seat at the scanning station on the bridge. Lestor would take on sickbay duties and become the acting scanning officer and the first officer. Lestor was already in Sickbay, cleaning up the bloody mess and preparing Torven's body for burial. He was glad he hadn't drawn that assignment.

The Captain was sitting in his command chair, watching a video feed of the alien from inside the airlock, when Major Bray stormed on deck.

"Captain, this alien gutted one of our crew and nearly killed two others in Engineering. He's a clear and present danger to this ship. I say we space him immediately."

Xander turned to look at Bray with steady gray eyes. "I have the final say around here, mister."

Bray snarled and started to pace around the tiny bridge. "Let me interrogate him them. Find out who he is and where he came from. Better yet, let me persuade him with pain."

"What will you ask him when you don't speak his language? Huh?" Xander shouted, pointing to the monitor.

Bray stopped and stared bitterly at the monitor. The alien was starting to slow down and wiggle less. Trying to conserve his energy.

"Then let me space him."

"That's murder," Vance offered, stepping into the fight.

"Is it? He killed Torven."

Xander sat up taller in his seat and said firmly, "No. This isn't an eye for an eye, Major."

Bray scoffed but didn't reply.

Boxer came onto the bridge and hovered just out of the way, but the Captain noticed her.

"Security, keep the airlock under guard twenty-four-seven until further notice," Xander ordered.

"Aye, sir. What about feeding him? We don't even really know what he is or what he eats."

Vance offered, "He seems like us in many ways. I'd bet he would drink water if we offered it to him."

Bray shook his head in disgust. "Space rations and only what you can squeeze through the transfer box."

Boxer looked to the Captain, who agreed with Major Bray. "Aye, sir."

Chapter 8

Lieutenant Vance stayed on the bridge at the Scanning Station. Assessing Torven's settings, he quickly found a new signal not far from their current location. It was a weak ELT (emergency locator transmitter) signal broadcasting on Federation frequencies. Vance isolated the signal and slipped on some headphones. He listened carefully to verify it.

"Captain, I've got an ELT signal near the gas giant. It's weak, but it matches Federation transmissions."

"Put it on speaker," Xander said.

The repeating high-frequency audible signal sounded eerie as it echoed off the metal walls of the tiny bridge. Xander nodded and then told him to cut it off with a swipe of his hand across his neck.

"Send the coordinates to Helm," Xander said. "Lestor, plot an intercept course."

"Aye, Captain."

The course change appeared on the primary monitor as a blue line heading for another, smaller moon of the gas giant. Xander punched his intercom. "Engineering, this is the Captain. We're changing orbits. Everything shipshape back there?"

There was a pause longer than usual from Engineering. Then Qin's raspy old voice responded. "We're good to go, Captain."

Xander waved to Lestor, who nodded back in her readiness. "Set course steady ahead, one quarter."

"Course set, one quarter ahead," Lestor replied.

The *Weippe* moved forward on the new course. Sunlight shifted through the portholes as they adjusted course. They held the course for several hours until reaching the smaller moon's range. Vance put the forward cameras on the primary monitor, and they could just make out the twisted remains of a starship hull reflecting starlight.

Captain Xander sipped a mug of coffee while watching the monitor. "Major Bray, report to the shuttle for a reconnaissance mission. Looks like we found the *Wayfarer*."

"Copy, Captain," Bray responded over the intercom.

Xander glanced at Lestor. "Sub Lieutenant, see if you can find any survivors—humans, not whatever the hell that alien is. If you don't find anything, hightail it back. I don't think we're alone out here. That man must have been part of a recent mission, or he would have been as dead as the humans he killed."

Lestor secured her station and left the bridge. Vance got up to come to the Captain's side. "Sir, permission to go with them?"

Xander looked at him for a moment, contemplating. "No, Number One. I need you on the scopes. I suspect whoever is out here will be showing themselves soon."

Vance nodded grimly. He was ready for a little payback.

***

It didn't take them long to get to the broken hull of the civilian starship in the shuttle. The *Wayfinder* hung awkwardly around the small gray moon in a low orbit. Its usually white exterior was scorched black from multiple hits by hostile fire. Nobody knew what kind of weapon was responsible, only that the result hadn't been good for the defenseless civilian starship.

The shuttle docked at the port-side airlock in short order. Rizzo and Bryant entered the ship, rifles raised and ready for attack. It took them several minutes to report back in, and Rizzo's voice sounded disgusted when they did. "Rec One, we're inside the galley, no signs of life. Bodies hacked up everywhere."

"Copy Rec One. Proceed with your sweep to the bridge," Bray said into his mic.

Lieutenant Lestor stayed strapped in her seat, using the shuttle's simple scanners to sweep space near them. She had a nervous feeling that something would happen, and it wouldn't go away. It felt as if they were being watched, but by whom and from where, she had no idea. Major Bray was behind her, watching his monitors, which were showing camera footage from both of his soldiers.

There continued to be nothing but cadavers as they swept from hallway to sub-corridor on their way to the bridge. Several blast holes caused them to go around the damaged areas. When they finally got to the bridge, it was completely blown away. No survivors.

"Nothing, sir. Shall we try Engineering?"

Bray grunted something that Lestor didn't understand. Whatever it was, Rizzo understood and kept moving. Major Bray unstrapped and started unpacking something from a container they had brought aboard before Lestor boarded. She looked over her shoulder and saw it was some kind of massive gun. But of course, soldiers were ever fascinated with bigger and worse guns.

Rizzo and Bryant reached Engineering and reported back — no survivors. "It looks like the nuclear drive was shut down and not destroyed. I don't see any damage here at all," Rizzo all but whispered.

"Like a slaughterhouse in here, clearly someone boarded her somewhere," Bryant offered.

***

Lieutenant Vance studied his scanner instruments, convinced they were not functioning correctly. The ELT signal did not originate from the *SS Wayfinder*. It was coming from a remote beacon—the type that was ejected from a ship when the captain was certain his ship would be destroyed. The beacon's long-duration battery broadcast a carrier signal over high-frequency radio waves.

The signal was nearby, but not coming from the dead hull of the ship. It had to be coming from beyond it. "Captain, I believe the ELT is coming from an emergency buoy, not the *Wayfinder*."

Captain Xander rubbed his gray beard as he thought. "Where is the buoy?"

Vance made another adjustment to triangulate the signal. He looked up and said, "From just beyond the visible horizon of the moon, sir."

Xander stood up and stepped toward the primary monitor that showed the scorched hulk of the *Wayfinder*. Vance watched him and wondered what the Captain was thinking. Xander slowly turned to face Vance. He looked spooked, as if he knew something wasn't quite right.

"Number One, I don't like this," Xander said, just loud enough to be heard.

***

Lestor pulled away from the *Wayfinder's* busted hull and spun around the axis of the dead starship. She wanted to assess the damage from the outside and inside. A blackened hole in the side was wide enough to drive the shuttle through. "Found their entry point. Stay clear of the port forward airlock. It's been completely blown out," Lestor said.

"Copy that," Rizzo replied over the comm.

Lestor rechecked her scanners, repositioning the shuttle to face outward. She felt the hairs on her arms rise under her suit. As the bright gray surface of the moon slowly rotated below them, a starship revealed itself from behind the horizon. Her dark eyes fixed on it, unable to truly grasp its size.

The motion alarms startled her, and she tried to speak but couldn't. Finally, Bray came over and stared out the window at the rust-colored ship. "Good God, what the hell is that?" he uttered.

Lestor found her voice. "*Weippe, Ericson.* Are you seeing that?"

Captain Xander's alarmed voice responded. "Get back here ASAP!"

Lestor responded immediately by heading to the airlock where they had deposited the soldiers. Bray pulled himself away from the window and started securing the weapon. He locked it to the deck on a low tripod that pointed out the back hatch.

"What's going on out there?" asked Rizzo.

"Get back to the entry point, Sergeant. We've got company," Bray said.

Lestor had the shuttle docked long before Rizzo and Bryant showed up. She monitored her scanners and received position updates as the alien ship revealed itself.

"ETA, *Ericson?*" Xander asked over the comm.

Lestor glanced at Bray, who was following their progress.

"Ten mike," Bray said, using the phonetic alphabet for brevity.

"Ten mike to boarding, gonna take us fifteen or more to get back," Lestor reported.

There was a long pause before Xander responded. "Don't delay."

***

Lestor disengaged the *Ericson* as quickly as she could. Fortunately, they were hidden from the view of the alien starship. But that also meant she couldn't see how close it was getting.

"*Weippe*, how far out is the alien ship?" she asked.

"Don't ask, just git."

The *Ericson's* engines strained under full thrust as Lestor took the most direct route back to the *Weippe*.

The shuttle suddenly shook violently, causing an alarm to flash as pressure was lost inside. Anything not attached or strapped in was blown out, leaving a gaping hole in the back. Lestor turned around to see what caused it. Major Bray was strapped to the big gun while Sergeant Rizzo was holding onto a seat strap for dear life, his legs dangling free. There was no sign of Sergeant Bryant.

"Lieutenant, we lost Bryant. Don't go back, repeat, don't go back for her," Bray screamed over the helmet comm.

Lestor saw a green blur zip past the open hole just as Bray opened up with his cannon. Flashes of light exploded inside the shuttle. Lestor turned around quickly and blinked hard to get rid of the spots blinding her vision. She fumbled with the controls as the spots faded. Several energy bursts on either side of her caused her to bank hard left and then right. Her stern scanners were offline, and she had no way of knowing whether she was evading the attacker.

"Take that, you sons of bitches!" Bray screamed like a madman.

The shuttle lurched again as it was hit by debris from the explosion behind them. Bray had hit his target. More maniacal screaming into her headphones as Lestor tried to raise the *Weippe*.

"*Weippe*, *Ericson*. Coming in hot. Lost starboard engine and everything else on my six."

"Copy, can you reduce approach speed?"

"I'll try. No guarantees."

Lestor shook her head in frustration as she jockeyed the controls. The shuttle was sluggish in its response. She had to make two turns before she was lined up to land in the shuttle bay. Unfortunately, her starboard thrusters were gone along with the engine. Which meant she could turn only in one direction. It left her no way to counter its port thrusters.

She turned back to face Rizzo, who had secured himself in a jump seat. "Sergeant, I need your help to steer us into the shuttle bay."

His eyes grew enormous behind the faceplate of his suit. He looked to the Major, who was still on the gun. He nodded to Rizzo. "What can I do, ma'am?"

Lestor turned her seat around to face Rizzo.

"There's a tank behind you. We'll vent it off into space to act like a thruster."

Rizzo looked over his shoulder and saw the access panel labeled HAZMAT DANGER - HYPERGOL PROPELLANT.

He looked back at the Lieutenant.

"Of course, it's hydrazine," he said.

She nodded slowly.

He frowned and said, "Okay, what do I do?"

"Open that panel and pull out the hose. It will have a nozzle at the end. I need you to point the end of the nozzle out of the starboard side. I can control the release of the fuel, but I need you to aim it outside, perpendicular to the ship."

Rizzo opened the panel and pulled out a length of hose. It was just barely long enough to reach. He had to walk along the shuttle's wall and reach over with his right hand to get the nozzle out of the back of the hatch.

Lestor returned to her controls and eased them into the final approach under the *Weippe*. "Are you good, Sergeant?"

"Name's Rizzo. I'm ready."

Lestor put a gloved forefinger over the release button and gently pushed it. The shuttle slid back onto a straight vector and started to go off enough for her to compensate with the port thruster. The shuttle slowly edged closer to the bay. It was an ugly approach. Coming in at a slight downward pitch, she got the shuttle into the safety net and shut down the power.

Turning around, she unstrapped to help Rizzo up from the jagged edge of the floor. "You did it, Rizzo, good job."

"Nice landing, ma'am. Glad I could help."

"You should go decon now. That stuff will eat into your suit."

Rizzo nodded and headed for decontamination. Major Bray was securing the cannon. He stopped and reached out a gloved hand to shake. Lestor hesitated, then took his hand.

"Not a bad bit of flying, LT."

Lestor frowned. "I'm sorry about your soldier. What happened to her?"

Bray looked at the hole in the shuttle as he spoke. "Bad luck. She was standing by the hatch when it blew. Didn't have a prayer."

"She might have survived the blast."

Bray shook his head. "I saw it happen. Her suit was compromised. If you don't mind, I'd like to forget that image."

Lestor didn't detect much regret from him, and that pissed her off. They lost someone, and all he seemed to care about was his damn gun. She was about to lay into him for his lack of compassion when the ship-wide alarms began sounding.

Chapter 9

Captain Xander stared obsessively at the alien ship on the main viewer. It was coming at them, and it slowly became clear just how massive it was. Xander unfolded a thin monitor in his chair and punched up all the data they had on the developing system.

"Quarter power to reverse. Back us slowly, Helm."

Lestor's replacement was an enlisted kid with glasses from engineering. "Aye, Captain, one-quarter reverse," he repeated.

"Number One, find me some cover. I'm not going toe to toe with that giant."

Vance was prepared for that. He had already scanned the space around them and determined the best hiding place. The gas giant planet had an icy ring that they could hide in.

"Navigation, set a course to the following coordinates," Vance said, sending them to Lestor, who had just arrived and relieved her replacement. She was still wearing the undergarments from the spacesuit, a light gray mesh material with woven coolant tubes.

"Stay inside that cleared-out area. We're small enough to maneuver, but they probably won't risk coming in after us."

"Aye, sir," she said curtly.

Xander turned around upon hearing her voice. "Lieutenant, good to have you back. What happened on the return?" Xander asked in his grandfatherly voice.

"Some kind of smaller vessel attacked us. It blew the back hatch off and took Sergeant Bryant with it," Lestor said. The anger in her tone was just below the boiling point. She noticed Lieutenant Boxer look up from her gunnery station, mouth open in shock.

Lestor returned her attention to the captain. "Major Bray engaged the alien vessel with his heavy gun and destroyed it. I was forced to land without my port engine."

Xander shook his head. "Dammit."

He turned around and stared back at the looming, rust-colored starship. There were glowing circles on either side of what looked like the bridge.

"Sir, she's powering up some kind of weapon," Vance warned.

"Full reverse, get us out of here, Lieutenant," Xander said. He punched the intercom button on his armrest. "Attention all hands, this is the Captain. Brace for impact."

He had gotten the words out sooner than the ship fired on them with expanding balls of glowing energy. The *Weippe* turned as sharply as she could, and by the time the rounds impacted them, the drive funnels had taken full impact. The ship shuddered and shook as the room lights flickered and then stayed off. Emergency bridge lights blinked on, casting the room in a soft red glow.

"Engineering, damage report," Xander hollered.

Vance and Lestor exchanged looks. The constant throb of the main drive was silent. The only noise came from the air circulation fans above them. A few instruments arced, and the crew quickly put out the fires with handheld fire extinguishers.

"Engineering to Bridge. The mains are out. I can give you maneuvering thrusters only," came the relatively calm voice of Qin over the intercom.

Xander waved at Lestor. "Go, get us moving!"

She punched her controls, and they limped away as fast as an old garbage scow.

"Boxer, get that top gun firing. I don't care if they are in range," Xander barked.

"Aye, Captain," she responded. Seconds later, you could hear the giant railgun loading, firing, and adjusting its aim to fire again. Steel rods exploded out of the twin barrels and punched toward the alien ship through the void. It seemed to Vance that it took forever to reach their target.

When they did, Vance was ready with a narrow scan of the enemy ship. He put a visual on the primary monitor, hoping to get a decent shot of them hitting home. Just before the rounds hit the enemy ship's hull, there was a flash. Vance figured that would have been their defensive electromagnetic shields. Then the rounds hit.

Several minor explosions were followed by chunks of metal flinging outward in random patterns. *They hit something, by God,* Vance thought.

"Direct hit, minimal damage, near as I can tell," he said.

Xander pounded a fist on his armrest pad. "Keep firing until we get out of range."

Boxer nodded, her fingers flexing over the commands at her console. The twin railguns fell silent as she recalculated the range for efficiency. "I need a slight port roll, please."

Lestor replied quickly, "Rolling port, two degrees."

"Gonna need four."

Lestor pushed her joystick over more until the ship was at the requested angle. "At four degrees port."

"Firing," Boxer stated as the guns spat more metal along their magnetic rails.

The *Weippe's* port side was exposed to the enemy, and they took a shot before the little Corvette could get behind the moon.

"Brace again," Captain Xander hollered.

The ship shuddered and then vibrated like a struck iron bell. The vibrations rattled the crew's teeth before dissipating.

"Damage report," Xander asked.

Boxer studied her status board and responded, "Direct hit to port airlock." She stopped when she realized what that meant.

Everyone looked at Xander, who nodded grimly and didn't say or do anything. The irony of their killing their own man was not lost on him. Neither was the satisfaction he felt.

"How soon until we are in the ring, Number One?"

Vance glanced at his orbital tracking graph. "At current maximum speed, five minutes, sir."

Xander stared at the massive alien ship getting bigger on the screen.

"Lieutenant Boxer. Please get your defense crew ready, just in case."

Boxer snapped a salute and hustled off the bridge. The same crewman who had manned Lestor's station took over for Boxer.

Vance felt a lump in his throat. Sweat beaded on his forehead. He quickly wiped it away with a sleeve. There was no way they could outrun that thing. It was just a matter of time before it caught up with them and similarly destroyed them. He had never been forced to consider his death before. They always had the upper hand whenever his previous assignments had engaged pirates. There was never any doubt who would win the engagement, and it built up an invincibility inside him he had been oblivious to until now.

"Time to the ring?" Captain Xander asked.

Vance refocused on his screen and tried to talk, but his throat was too dry. Finally, he managed to utter, "Two minutes, sir."

"Time until their weapons intercept us?"

Vance froze. He couldn't speak. Lestor jumped in with a quick response.

"Thirty seconds, Captain."

Xander was too focused on the orange ship to care who answered him. Vance pulled a water bottle from under his station and took a swig. His eyes were still on the alien ship as it closed in on them. The details were clearer now as it filled the main viewer.

Everything about it screamed war, from the menacing shape of its angular lines to the endless arrays of probes and weapons that pointed at them like an angry porcupine. It was easily three times bigger than they were. This must be what a grouper feels like as a shark approaches out of the murky depths.

A warning flashed on Vance's screen. They were within firing range again. The alien ship could start blasting them into cosmic particles at any moment.

"They're in range to fire, Captain," Vance managed to say.

It was deathly quiet on the bridge.

Chapter 10

ance looked from the Captain to the main viewer. Nothing happened. He could hear the thrusters burning and wondered how long they would hold. The digital clock ticked down. Seconds remained before they would be in the thick of the nebula. New data streamed across his monitors.

"Ring composition analysis, Captain. Mostly ice and methane. Thirty percent rock and miscellaneous metals. Nothing over a few meters in diameter," Vance read aloud.

Captain Xander pointed to the alien ship. It was slowing.

"They don't seem interested in chasing us. Why?"

New data streamed across Vance's scanners. He tweaked the numbers and then looked up at the Captain. "Lots of radiation out there, Captain. This area is right in the middle of the electromagnetic field of the gas giant, and it generally has deadly radiation belts."

Xander wiped thoughtfully at his gray beard as he looked at the viewscreen that showed the edge of the ring. Wisps of tiny ice crystals lingered around the ring like smoke clouds.

"How long can we safely stay in here, Number One?"

Vance checked the concentration levels and then made some quick calculations. "Not recommended for more than a couple of hours, sir."

Xander punched the intercom button on his armrest. "Qin, how long until you can get the main online?"

There was a long pause, as if Qin were too busy to answer. Finally, the speaker sputtered, and his voice spoke. "Six hours, tops."

Xander and Vance exchanged looks, and Vance slowly shook his head. That was too long. "You have two hours, Engineering. Captain, out."

Vance lifted an eyebrow. Xander brushed off the seemingly impossible timetable for the repair. "He always overestimates. He'll have them back on before we have to leave. In the meantime, get me a new hiding place, Lieutenant."

Vance nodded, "Aye, sir."

He called the system map again and noticed new details about the nearby gas giant. "New data on that gas giant, sir. High concentrations of ammonia, ammonium hydrosulfide, and water."

Vance looked up and shrugged. "Nothing unique there, typical gas ball."

Xander nodded as he returned his attention to the alien ship on the primary monitor. "Get down to engineering and see what you can do to help Qin," Xander said.

Lieutenant Vance stood up and headed aft. As he made his way down the narrow corridors, he heard Captain Xander's ship-wide announcement: "Attention, the ship. This is the Captain. We have two hours to get this ship ready for the next fight. All hands to the damaged areas for work details, Captain, out."

***

Engineering was a mess. Pipes and conduits littered the floor, and enlisted ratings immediately moved to and fro. Vance found Qin underneath the main drive, spot-welding something. He waited for the man to finish and then poked his head over the edge of the access panel on the floor. Qin was inside, straddling a large pipe, welder's goggles on, drenched in sweat.

"Captain asked me to lend a hand," Vance said.

Qin shook his head. "Got no time for that, Lieutenant. Just let my people do what we do. If I need something, I'll let you know."

Vance frowned. He was looking forward to getting his hands dirty. There had to be something he could do. "Are you sure, sir?"

Qin pulled one side of his goggles up. His dark eye squinted up at Vance.

"You still here?"

Vance backed away, hands up in surrender. An enlisted man replaced him and handed an instrument down to Qin, who grunted something unrecognizable. Vance patted the kid on the back and went forward to check on the battle damage.

The corridor was sealed off when he got to the port-side airlock. He peered through the glass window on the hatch and saw that the hull was breached right where the airlock was. *The alien was killed by his own people!* He stepped away from the hatch and found an intercom panel. "Vance went to the bridge. It looks like the hit to our port side took out the airlock. Our guest didn't make it."

Captain Xander's voice replied. Vance could hear the irritation despite the tiny speaker. "We know, Lieutenant. I thought you were in Engineering."

"Yes, sir. Commander Qin refused my help, sir. I thought I'd walk the ship and see if I could help with battle damage."

There was a longer-than-usual pause before the Captain replied.

"Carry on, Number One."

Vance smiled to himself. He finally did something right around here. He headed off toward the center of the ship to get around the damaged areas. When he arrived at the next bulkhead, a handful of ratings were helping to seal off the corridor by welding the hatch shut and closing air vents—standard procedure until they could get back to the space dock.

"Did anyone find the remains of our prisoner before you sealed off the corridor?" Vance asked the group. Everyone shook their heads.

"Okay, proceed as you were. Let me know if you need anything."

The nearest NCO replied, "Aye, sir."

Vance continued forward. Passing into Officer Country, he noticed Lieutenant Lestor pop out of her room and nod for him to join her. He followed her and said, "Shouldn't you be on the bridge?"

She was just finishing changing into her gray duty uniform, sliding on her boots. "I had to change. Listen, I'm getting the impression Major Bray knows more about these aliens than he's letting on."

Vance encouraged her to continue. She secured her boot and lowered her voice as she approached him. "I saw the look on his face when he shot that enemy ship out the back of the shuttle. It was pure rage. Like you'd expect someone to act who was seeking revenge."

"Didn't he lose a soldier? That would piss me off."

"No, it was different. I asked him about that, and he acted like her death was the price of doing business. I think they've gone up against the Blue-Devils before. Did you see all the weapons they brought with them? No Surface Army contingent is that well armed for duty on a Corvette."

Vance considered what she was saying for a moment. He had gotten the same impression, although he hadn't thought about it since they arrived in-system.

"Have you noticed how obsessed the Captain is with that alien ship? All he ever does is stare at it on the screen," Vance said.

Lestor nodded slowly. She had noticed. "I don't think we can beat that thing."

Vance met her dark eyes. Her brow was wrinkled with concern. He hadn't been this close to her before. She had flawlessly smooth brown skin without wrinkles or excessive makeup. He could smell her, and it was not unpleasant. Something inside him wanted to project his confidence. His chest expanded, and he tried his best not to appear worried.

"Look, we'll get out of this. I have complete faith in Qin to restore the mains, and then we can start dishing it back to them."

She rolled her big eyes and smiled. "You're full of shit, sir."

He laughed unexpectedly.

"Hey, no time for hanky-panky, you two," Lieutenant Boxer said from the doorway.

"We were just discussing Major Bray's behavior," Lestor said.

Boxer looked back out into the hallway and came inside, interested to learn what they had been discussing.

"The man's insane, isn't he?" Boxer asked.

Lestor grinned as she and Vance nodded in agreement.

"He's taking this fight way too personally."

Boxer nodded. "So, I'm not the only one who noticed that."

"Trin thinks he's fought the aliens before," Vance said.

Boxer's eyes brightened. "I know. Did you see all the toys they brought with them? Some of their weapons I've never even seen before. I think one of the boxes in the shuttle bay is a nuke. It's damn insane."

That was news to both Lestor and Vance. "Wait, how do you know that for sure?" Vance asked.

"I've seen it opened when they were cleaning and didn't think I'd notice. There was a nuclear radiation sticker inside the lid of the case. Normally, they have to placard the outside, too."

Vance seemed to zone out. The two women looked at him and then at each other.

"Vance?" Lestor asked.

He didn't respond, still lost in thought.

"Lieutenant, you still with us?" Boxer said, waving her hand before his face. Vance blinked and looked at her.

"Sorry, I was just thinking about that weapon. Why would they bring it aboard and keep it a secret?"

Boxer sighed. "It's the freaking Army, man. They're some kind of secret squirrel outfit. Won't even let me get near their stuff."

Vance looked at Lestor. Her dark eyes were wide, as if she were expecting him to say something.

"Look, we just have to do our jobs and not try to second guess anyone—least of all the Captain or Major Bray," Vance said, eyeing both women.

Lestor frowned, and Boxer shook her head.

"What?" Vance asked.

"I thought you were going somewhere, sir," Lestor admitted.

"Me too."

Vance looked at Boxer. "When we leave this ring and clear the radiation belt, that alien ship will be all over us. If the Army has a weapon that can help, we will use it. Otherwise, there's only so long we can hold them off."

"Are you saying we don't stand a chance?" Boxer said, her hands on her hips.

"I didn't say that."

"But you implied it, sir."

Vance stared back at her and didn't respond.

****

Lieutenant Vance rapped on the Captain's cabin door twice. "Enter," Xander said from inside.

Vance let himself in and stood at attention. Xander was sitting at his table, staring at his monitor. "At ease, Number One."

Vance dropped into a relaxed stance with his hands behind his back. Captain Xander motioned for him to sit down on his bunk. Vance did so reluctantly. He always found sitting with a Captain too personal, as if his superior should never be on the same level as him. It was an oddity, but that's just how he felt.

"Armon, I wanted to apologize for my behavior on the bridge. I've been a bit curt with everyone, especially you. I guess I'm just feeling the pressure. I've never encountered anyone like the Blue-Devils in my years in deep space. I don't know how we'll get out of this alive. The minute we leave hiding, they will pounce on us like a tiger."

Vance was uncomfortable now. His captain was admitting weakness to him, and that was unnerving. Captains were supposed to always have the answers, and when they didn't, they were never allowed to admit it. *This guy's coming unglued*, he thought.

Xander looked at him with tired eyes. "I know I'm not supposed to admit defeat, but this bastard stumps me. What say you? Do you have any ideas?"

Vance shrugged. *What did he expect me to know if a thirty-year veteran couldn't figure it out?* He thought.

"No, sir."

Xander frowned and said, "I'm sure something will present itself. In the meantime, keep me apprised of what your scans find. That is all."

Vance stood and started to leave but then stopped.

"Captain, I'm sure we'll find a way out. The crew and I are behind you a hundred percent."

Xander nodded and waved his hand as Vance left.

Chapter 11

Lieutenant Vance shuffled off to the head for a shower after his shift. He was overdue for a good cleaning and could no longer stand himself. Someone was using the far stall when he stepped inside the cramped bath. There was a modest privacy wall between the showerheads, but it wasn't enough to hide behind. Most people just did their business and hardly spoke to each other.

As he took off his robe and hung it up, he noticed it was Lieutenant Lestor in the other stall. She was rinsing off as he was lathering up. Their eyes met briefly, and she smiled politely at him. He wasn't in the mood for play and doubted she was interested in him, just being pleasant. Social courtesies were never a big priority for Vance unless he was after someone or something.

He scrubbed himself well and let the warm water fall across his face. The sound of the water splashing on the metal floor lulled him into a drowsy state. He didn't hear her toweling off behind him, or he would've found some excuse to turn around and check her out. She had left before he pulled his head out of the stream, and the water cut off.

The hatch opened as he was drying off, and in stepped Lieutenant Boxer. She was naked and carried her towel. He glanced at her as she passed, but she ignored him. He smiled and put on his robe. *If only.*

"You guys didn't use all the hot water, did you?" Boxer said, turning on the water.

Vance glanced over at her nude back. *Damn, she was fine. Too bad.*

"Nope, left you your five minutes worth," he said as he opened the hatch.

The next thing he knew, a sudden shudder left them both sprawled out on the floor. "What the hell was that?" Boxer asked. She hadn't even had a chance to lather up. Lying sprawled out naked on the cool metal floor, she held on, palms down as the ship rumbled.

"Attention, the ship. We have a hull breach. Deck two forward," the Captain said over the ship's PA.

Vance helped Boxer up, who pushed him away when she had gotten to her feet. Lieutenant Lestor showed up in the corridor half-dressed and handed them their pistols. Boxer took the gun, checked it for ammo, and then tied her towel around her. "That's just a few meters down, safeties off," she said.

Vance followed the security officer and shouted at Lestor, "Get to the bridge. Tell them we're heading to the breach."

"Aye."

Lestor went down the corridor opposite the staircase that led up one floor to the bridge. Vance followed Boxer around the corner, where she had frozen in place. She pointed to the object in the outboard wall behind Vance's cabin.

"Wanna bet that's a bomb?" Boxer asked.

Vance shook his head as they ducked back around the corner, breathing heavily from the adrenaline rush.

"Could be a breaching device," Vance replied. He stepped back through the nearest bulkhead, and they secured the door.

"Captain, this is Vance. We've shut off the corridor on deck two, starboard. A suspected breaching device is in the hull behind my cabin."

Xander's scratchy voice responded. "Is that deck evacuated?"

Vance and Boxer looked at each other and shrugged. All the officers in this section were on duty, so there was the possibility that a steward might be in the wardroom.

"I'll check the ward for enlisted," Vance replied.

Vance opened the hatch again, spinning the locking mechanism with a few quick pulls. He handed Boxer his pistol and tightened the towel around his waist. This is stupid, he thought. There had better be someone in there.

"Secure the hatch when you get into the wardroom in case that thing goes off," Boxer warned him.

Vance nodded and walked cautiously around the corner as Boxer secured the hatch again. Seeing no change in the device, he padded to the wardroom hatch and stepped inside, closing it behind him. Eyes darting around, he hollered, "Anyone in here?"

Nobody responded as he moved into the cramped closeted area where the stewards prepared drinks. There was broken glass on the floor, and he stopped short of it. One of the wine bottles had been left on a metal counter, and the jolt had knocked it to the floor. Red wine had spilled like thin blood across the floor. Vance went to the porthole on the port side and tried to look left to where the device was, but couldn't see it. What he did see alarmed him further.

Dozens of space-suited aliens slowly approached from behind the icy chunks of the inner belt. It was like an old drama where the bad guys slowly advanced through the fog of a battlefield.

"Bridge, Vance. We have incoming hostiles on the port side. Nobody in the wardroom, heading back out."

"Copy, Lieutenant," Xander responded.

The aliens were too small and traveled in irregular patterns, which Vance knew would have tricked the scanners into thinking they were just chunks of rotating ice.

Out in the corridor, he looked over at the alien device. Something made him approach it slowly. It was a strange blue-gray color, and he noticed it had a brushed metal texture on the nose cone, which was all that was visible. He could smell the acrid stench of space and knew the seal between the void and the cabin pressure was tenuous at best, but still, he lingered.

Vance reached out with his right hand to touch it. The damn thing punched its way through solid deck metal. It won't be pressure-sensitive. The metal was cool to the touch, as he expected. What he didn't expect - it moved. He felt like he could maybe just push it out of the hole it made. He didn't put any more pressure on it and quickly stepped back. The metal of the old ship creaked, and for a second, he thought the alien device would slide out, but it remained. Vance tightened the towel around his waist and turned to leave. If it hadn't gone off yet, there was a good chance they were waiting until they got closer to detonate it.

Then he remembered his clothes were in his room. He had nothing to wear but the damn small towel. He glanced over at his cabin door and then back to the device. There wasn't any time. A thought struck him, and he returned to the main corridor and paused. *Who else could be around here?* He couldn't find anywhere to check, so he returned the way he came. Boxer let him back in, and they both locked the hatch.

"The aliens are coming across the ring in spacesuits. You'd better get your people ready."

Boxer grimaced, then looked down at him and said, "You can use one of Torvin's uniforms since your cabin is occupied." Vance agreed, and they retreated to Torvin's cabin. He quickly found a pair of pants and a shirt while Boxer dressed in her adjoining cabin. The pants were too tight. He didn't realize Torvin was that small around the waist. He pulled them off and searched through the dead man's possessions until he found a pair of Fleet sweatpants. Stepping into them, they were tight but wearable.

Boxer came back into the entrance fully dressed. She had to grin at the too-tight t-shirt and barely fitting pants. "Guess he was smaller than I remembered," she said.

"There's a spacesuit rack up one deck. I'll grab one of them."

They parted ways as they left the cabins, Boxer going aft to get her security troops on station and Vance heading up to the bridge.

***

By the time Lieutenant Vance reached the bridge, he was wearing a space suit and carrying a helmet. Captain Xander was standing at the porthole, looking out at the approaching aliens. He motioned for Vance to join him.

"Lieutenant, how do you suggest we fight them off? I'm seeing dozens of them, and nearly all carry some weapon."

When Vance didn't answer, Xander looked at him.

"That device on deck two is a breaching tool. I think they just pull it out and crawl in. It fits with what Lestor said they saw on the *Wayfinder*."

Vance noticed the Captain's eyes grow slightly larger as he listened. Then he looked back out the round porthole.

"I don't understand why they don't change their angle and come at us from above the ring. Instead of sneaking through the ice debris and attacking in suits."

Lestor had quietly joined them. Her dark eyes were almost as large as the Captain's. "Hard to imagine a space-faring race not thinking in three dimensions."

Xander shook his head. "Not to mention their ship is so big, it could just plow through the ice and hit us physically."

Major Bray and Sergeant Rizzo entered the bridge, weapons at the ready and armor clanking.

"Captain, I've mounted my Maser cannon in the shuttle bay. If you can yaw the ship, we can just sit back and pick those bastards off individually."

Vance looked at Rizzo, who nodded as if the plan were sound. Xander said to Lestor, "Do it."

"Aye, Captain."

Bray turned on his heels and left as quickly as he had come. Vance and Xander exchanged looks. "Better tell Boxer and her people to stand to, in case any get through."

Chapter 12

The ship stayed at action stations as the shuttle bay door opened. Major Bray and Sergeant Rizzo manned the maser cannon, with Bray as the spotter and Rizzo on the trigger. The shuttle parked off to the side was there in case they needed cover.

Ice clumps floated a few hundred meters away, wisps of vapor radiating outward from the nearby star's heat. Slowly, the *Weippe* rotated around to face the incoming hostiles. Rizzo flipped off the safety and brought the weapon to bear on the closest target.

"Fire when ready, Sergeant," Bray said over the helmet comm.

Rizzo nodded inside his helmet and pulled the trigger. The cannon flash from the barrel was brilliant enough to illuminate the shuttle bay as it flung a bolt of energy into the void. The target alien disappeared in a dark cloud of blood.

"Nice shot," Bray praised as incoming streaks of light zipped past them from the alien's weapons. The shots reduced the far wall of the bay to molten rubble.

Rizzo acquired the next target and continued to pick off the aliens as they slowly advanced like some kind of ancient video game. He was taking care of business. There was no sound and only a distant puff of evaporated alien to satisfy his emotional need to exact revenge for Bryant's death.

"Helm, give us a few reverses to throw them off," Bray said.

The *Weippe* rotated back and then up and down again like the deck of a pitched boat on the open ocean. Enemy shots hit all around them. Rizzo had to aim against the motion, but it wasn't difficult for him. He started getting into a rhythm even as the aliens grew more prominent the closer they came.

"Like fish in a barrel, sir," he commented.

That's when he noticed the Major was no longer beside him. He had taken multiple hits from the enemy weapons and was ripped in half across the upper torso. Gravity had been cut to the bay to make it harder for the attackers to gain a foothold, and the Major's slain form floated away from Rizzo in slow motion.

"Major Bray is down, repeat, Bray is down. They're getting too close for my cannon. I'm bailing," Rizzo stated excitedly as he pushed off for the shuttle. He had a rifle slung over his shoulder. He pulled it up, pointed it at the nearest attacker, and shot. The rounds were designed to fire in space and had depleted-uranium heads. The alien's spacesuit was punctured easily, and he veered away into one of his fellow soldiers. That bought Rizzo enough time to reach the shuttle for cover.

"Could use some backup out here," Rizzo shouted into his helmet comm.

The nearest hatch swung open, and several spacers shot out, firing their much more primitive rifles at the attackers. One of them took a headshot and drifted away in a cloud of red. The second one was Lieutenant Boxer, her weapon the same as Rizzo's.

"Get inside, Sergeant!"

Rizzo squeezed a few more shots and pushed off for the open hatch. Boxer's suit had a simple maneuvering system attached, and she was able to retreat after him, laying down cover fire.

"We have a hull breach on deck two," Captain Xander's voice announced.

"Shit," Boxer said as she Rizzo locked the hatch.

Peering through the thick glass window of the bay, she could see several more aliens entering the bay. She started lowering the bay door when Rizzo took over. "I got this, ma'am."

Boxer nodded and started to run back towards the front of the ship. Rizzo watched her leave and then readied himself for another fight.

***

By the time Boxer got to the forward section of the *Weippe*, the aliens were already inside and trying to blast through the hatch that Vance had secured. She slowly advanced down the corridor with her rifle at the ready. A movement on the stairs caught her eye. It was Vance coming down, still dressed in his suit. She waited for him to join her. All he had was a pistol.

"Here," she said, taking a larger sub-rifle off her shoulder and handing it to him. "Just spray and pray, sir."

He grinned nervously back at her inside his helmet.

The hatch exploded, and white-hot metal was flung at them down the corridor. Boxer started shooting at the hole with her rifle. Smoke from the explosion flew back out of the ship toward the breach. The alien intruders didn't advance. Boxer motioned that she was going to move in. Vance covered her the best he could.

When Boxer reached the hatch, there were no bodies. Vance came up beside her and peered into the empty corridor.

"They must have gotten blown back out when this hatch gave way."

"What the hell?" Boxer asked rhetorically.

Vance shrugged. "Let's secure this area and get back to the shuttle bay. Rizzo's all alone back there."

Vance nodded, and Boxer squeezed through the hole without touching the still-warm metal. She quickly advanced around the bend to where the original breach was.

"The device is gone. Follow me," Boxer urged.

Vance stepped through the hole in the hatch and moved to the wall beside her. Sure enough, there was a gaping hole where an alien metal device once existed. Boxer quickly passed the hole and up the hall to the Captain's room. Vance stayed put, ensuring nobody came from the wardroom or the other cabin up the hall from him. Boxer came back quickly and gave him the thumbs-up. She quickly checked the wardroom and came back with another gloved thumbs up. They cleared the remaining cabins on the starboard side and fell back through the destroyed hatch.

"Maintenance crew to deck two forward, starboard. We need to get a hatch welded shut. The ship is clear." Vance ordered through the suit comm.

The Captain's voice echoed the command. Vance turned to Boxer, who had already started heading back down the dimly lit main corridor leading to the main body of the tiny ship.

Vance decided there was no reason to stick around and followed after Boxer. He figured his chances of surviving a firefight might increase if he were with her and Rizzo.

***

The fight was over when Vance got to the shuttle bay. The Surface Army soldier was conferring with

Lieutenant Boxer in the corridor with one of the Boxer's ratings nearby.

"SITREP?" Vance asked.

"The Major's dead, and so is one of my kids. But the bay doors are closed, and the area secure," Boxer said.

The soldier looked as if he wanted to say something.

"Go ahead, Sergeant."

"Someone has to go out there and ensure the ship's clean. Who knows what they left on the hull, sir," Rizzo said wearily.

Vance looked at Boxer. "Negative. The radiation is too intense. We're going to be pushing off soon, hopefully."

"Sir, what if there are more hostiles on the hull?" Boxer's hair was wet from sweating in her helmet. Vance tried not to recall what she looked like sprawled out naked on the grated floor in the shower.

"Then they will die of radiation exposure, not us."

He looked back at Rizzo.

"We need to secure the hull breach on two forward. Can you help with that? Make sure the techs have cover?"

Rizzo nodded slowly and confidently. Vance clapped his shoulder and said, "Outstanding."

He looked over at Boxer. "Keep me informed." Then he headed aft to check on the progress in Engineering.

***

Engineering was starting to look normal again to Vance's untrained eye. It was still a rusted old bucket of scrap metal compared to every other ship in the fleet, but he was slowly beginning to appreciate the old girl. She'd been shot at and skewered by a breaching probe and hadn't given up her ghost yet. So maybe there was still a chance they'd all get back to Federation space.

"How are repairs coming, Commander?" Vance asked as the old man came around the intermixer pipes.

Qin was sweaty, and his face and hands were marked with grease. His normally clean and neat uniform was equally filthy. "We're close, Lieutenant. But we need another hour or so," Qin sighed.

Vance was okay with that. It would give his hull repair crews some time.

"Okay, thanks for your efforts, sir. Let me know if I can get you any help."

Qin managed a thin smile and turned back to his charges.

Vance left Engineering and found an intercom link to the bridge back in the ship's main body. "Captain Vance."

"Go."

"Engineering's going to need another hour. I've got a repair crew going outside to fix the breach, and Boxer's people will cover them. Major Bray is KIA, and I saw at least two other bodies in the shuttle bay. We're going to need a mortuary crew."

There was a pause before Captain Xander replied. *He's probably issuing orders.*

"Okay, Vance. Get back up here," Xander finally responded.

"Aye, sir."

On his way forward and up to the bridge, Vance passed several enlisted hustling by on their way either to repair the ship or reclaim the dead. For the first time, he felt like he was on a warship, at war. The Federation had never been in a protracted war before. Their fleet was small, only a dozen ships of various classes, and no living captain or crew had ever been to war.

Those fresh young faces that passed him were just as scared as he was, but they didn't show it. All he saw was a grim determination to do their jobs so they could all make it home alive. It made him proud to be their commander. Sure, their ship was junk, and their captain was over the hill, but the crew was strong and confident of their abilities. He raised his head higher and took the narrow stairs to the bridge level.

Chapter 13

On the bridge, Vance set his helmet on the scanner console and stood beside the captain in his chair. Xander's face was drawn, and there were bags under his eyes when he looked at Vance.

"How long for repairs?"

Vance glanced at the chronograph embedded in his suit arm. "About an hour; after that, we'll need to get the hell out of this radiation."

"I have something I want to discuss with you. Come with me," Xander said as he got up and headed for the back of the bridge. The Captain's Mast room was just off the bridge and was big enough for maybe four people. Used for doling out punishment to the crew when needed, Xander liked to use it for private conversations. There was a simple metal table and two stiff back chairs. The room's back wall was an access panel that led to the instrument racks housing communications and scanning gear.

After Vance shut the hatch, Xander began.

"Have you ever been to sea? You know, like the navies of the past?"

Vance shook his head no. *Where the hell is he going with this?*

Xander took a moment to frame his thoughts before beginning.

"Naval ships mostly ran on top of the water. But there used to be specialized ships that ran underneath the waves. They called them..."

"Submarines, yes, I know this," Vance interjected.

"Right. Subs were pressurized, not unlike starships. But they were not designed for deep-water use. So if they happened to go too deep, they would implode from the pressure of the outside water."

Vance nodded. Xander moved to the single porthole and pointed to the gas giant outside. "The atmosphere of a Jovian planet is just like deep water. The lower in the clouds you go, the higher the pressure. At some point, gases even turn to liquid."

Vance looked out at the swirling bands of orange and white gas of the planet's atmosphere. He wasn't entirely tracking.

"If we dive into the planet's upper atmosphere, the Blue-Devils might follow us," Xander said, his voice trailing off as he tried to lead Vance to his idea.

Vance shook his head. "But a starship's not as thick-walled as a submarine; we'd be crushed."

"Exactly!"

"I don't follow you, sir."

"How far down into the atmosphere do you think they would go if they tried to follow us?"

Vance slowly started to catch on. "But we'd be crushed before them."

Xander winced. "That's where my plan breaks down. How do we trick them into sinking far enough to implode without actually popping ourselves?"

Vance shook his head. The whole idea seemed insane to him.

"Sir, we're repairing a breach in our hull. I'm unsure we could sustain that pressure even before the damage."

Xander waved his hand excitedly. "I know, I know, but I have this feeling that captain," he pointed behind them at the unseen enemy vessel, "will follow us wherever we go. His thinking is completely two-dimensional. Why didn't he simply come at us from above while we've been in this ring? Instead, he sends his men through the ring ice to attack us. That's crazy. It exposes them to radiation, and it's not efficient."

"I agree."

"So that tells me he's more emotional than logical. I bet he would chase us to a star if we led him there."

The two men looked at each other momentarily, and then Xander waved his hand. "No, I'm not going to start star diving."

Vance moved away in thought. "We need to trick them into going lower into the depths. They would have to track us somehow. We're running a nuclear drive, so they'd lock onto our radiological signature because I don't think they could get a visual on us in the storms."

Xander's eyes grew larger as he fed off Vance's idea. "If we went in at the pole, they'd have to contend with more radiation belts and probably massive lightning storms."

Vance held up a finger before the captain. "Right. We'd have to find a way to mask our stardrive's radiation signature."

"We could shut it down."

Vance shook his head. "Too risky."

"Is it?"

Xander had a half-mad glint in his eye as he countered. "We could go on battery power for life support. Shut down all active scanning."

Vance was slowly buying into the plan, as crazy as it sounded.

"We still need to convince them that we've gone lower… I got it!"

Xander saw the smile growing on Vance's face. "What?"

"We use Major Bray's maser gun."

Xander paused. "Shoot them with it?"

"No, let it overload and shove it out of the bay. Gravity will force it to drop like a rock, creating a radiation plume so bright they'd have to follow it."

Captain Xander raised his arms out with a huge, wide grin. "That's it!" He grabbed Vance's broad shoulders and shook him with excitement.

Then he let go and straightened himself. "Do you know why you were chosen for this mission?"

Vance's smile faded. He had always assumed it was because he had pissed off someone higher than him in the food chain.

"No, sir."

Xander's smile faded but did not leave his face.

"Admiral Drake hand-picked you."

Vance was dumbstruck. He'd never known any admirals, much less the dean of the Academy where he graduated.

"I don't understand, sir. Why?"

"She told me you were the most original thinker to ever pass through the Academy. I wanted someone with at least as much fleet experience as Ganner, but she gave me you instead. I studied your record. Fifth in his class, served on a light Destroyer and did some ground time at a depot. Frankly, son, you were about as wet behind the ears as a first-year graduate."

Vance's career seemed to be fine until he got assigned here. He wouldn't be the youngest officer to make flag rank, but he didn't care about being a fast riser, unlike some people he knew. He just wanted to get on a capital ship or a decent Destroyer. Bide his time until he made captain. Ever since he was a kid, he had wanted to be a captain. His family was poor, and he had no political connections. Just getting into the Academy had been challenging enough for him. He barely got through prep school with the help of several tutors and many late-night cramming sessions. Once in though, he held his own and graduated higher than anyone expected. He was proud of that.

"Admiral Drake took me to the club and bought me enough rounds to convince me to take you on. She said that of all the top graduates in your class, you were the only one who thought outside the normal conventions. I didn't see any evidence of that in your record. I thought she was setting me up for something."

Xander put a hand on Vance's shoulder.

"I was an idiot. Your performance so far has been much better than I anticipated. She was right. You do think outside the box. We'll need all the help we can get to make it home on this one."

Vance felt a bit like someone had kicked him in the nuts, but he was praised for not passing out.

"I'll put together a team to work out the details, sir."

Xander nodded and let go of him.

"Anything else, sir?"

Xander shook his head and followed Vance back out to the bridge.

Chapter 14

Repairs were underway when Lieutenant Vance brought two officers to the kitchen for an impromptu meeting. Deck two forward was still depressurized, and Vance wanted to brainstorm fixing it. Qin was brought in mainly because of his experience. He wouldn't take time away from his job unless fed tea. Well aware, Cook Odem brought him a tea bag and hot water as they all sat at the metal table.

"Thanks, son," Qin said.

"Just let me know if I can get anything else," Odem said as he returned to his cooking duties.

Lieutenant Lestor sat opposite Vance and Qin. Her hair was frayed, and her spacesuit was worn from helping with the repairs. She sipped water from a narrow thermos.

"The captain has a plan for defeating the alien ship. But it's going to require more modifications to survive."

Lestor popped her mouth off the thermos. "That doesn't sound promising."

Vance kept up his enthusiasm for the idea as he explained.

"We will head for the gas giant and descend into its atmosphere. He's sure the aliens will follow us. Once we get into the storms, we're going to shut down our reactor and drop the Major's nuclear gun. The aliens should lose us in the clouds and follow the radiological signature of the gun until they implode."

Qin and Lestor looked at each other, and both shook their heads.

"That's the plan?" Lestor asked.

Vance nodded.

"I just got my drive online. I'm not risking a shutoff until we're home."

Vance was ready for some resistance, especially from Qin.

"We have to go to reserve power and stay there until they take the bait. If the nuclear fire is burning, they don't buy it."

Qin took a long drink and didn't say anything more. Vance suspected he knew the shutdown was necessary but was too tired to argue.

"What can we do to make the hull stronger? We have to survive more pressure than the ship was designed for."

Lestor shook her head, clearly frustrated by the idea. "I don't know. The safest thing to do is get everyone in the ship's center and reinforce the hatches. How are you going to lower the gun to simulate our descent? If you just toss it out, it will fall too fast."

"I was hoping you could pilot the shuttle remotely and set it on a slow descent to simulate our mass."

Lestor nodded slowly. "I can do that, provided the storms don't interfere with my signal. It might be safer to lock in a course and let it go."

Vance agreed. "Perfect. Can you make it happen?"

She looked at him wearily. "You'll have to supervise the hull repairs. I'll need Rizzo's help with the gun."

"Not a problem. Qin, can you get us to the planet at full speed? We won't have much time to get there before they overtake us."

Qin set down his empty cup and sighed. "I'll give you what I can."

Vance frowned, but he knew that was all the old man was going to front him on this one. He looked back at Lestor. "I'm gonna need you at the helm until we get into position."

Lestor took another sip of water and nodded.

"Okay, let's get going then. We have about twenty minutes before we all start glowing," Vance said.

***

Lieutenant Vance arrived at the site where the hull had been breached and immediately saw the new hole in his cabin wall. They had cut out nearly half his wall to cover the hole in the ship's side.

"Who authorized this?" he asked.

The nearest tech was a young man with big eyes. When he recognized the first officer, he stood up. "Lieutenant Lestor, sir."

Vance walked into his cabin through the hole and looked around. They had removed what little he had brought.

"Where did she put my stuff?"

"All of your items were stowed in Commander Qin's cabin, sir," the kid said.

Vance turned around and came back out into the corridor. The hull plating was about twice as thick as the metal used for his cabin wall. He found the NCO in charge and approached him.

"I hope you have another layer outside," Vance said.

"Aye, sir," he replied with a thumb over his shoulder.

The inner wall of the airlock behind him was mainly gone, as if someone had removed it to access the machinery behind it. Vance moved over to the cut-out area and saw the thickness of the metal.

"Was this your idea?"

"No sir, but it was my handiwork."

Vance clapped his gloved hand on the man's back. "Outstanding!"

The man's smile was visible inside his helmet visor. Vance pulled him aside, even though their conversation was not private.

"Can you think of any other parts of this ship that might need to be reinforced with thicker plates? We're about to go diving like a sub. What areas could use some reinforcement?"

The man's smile faded as he thought about it.

"I need to keep us from popping as we sink into that gas giant's atmosphere," Vance prodded.

The man bobbed his head, getting a clearer picture of his commanding officer's question. "Well, sir, off the top of my head, I'd say the area above our heads is about the weakest skin of the ship," he said, pointing up.

Vance figured the bow would lose pressure first, but he knew the bridge would be okay. A tub of carbon fiber and metal surrounded it. They would evacuate the rest of the forward section into the main body. That left engineering cut off from the others but was well shielded.

"Okay, that's what I thought. When you guys restore the air in here, seal off the main body as well as you can. Remove whatever you have to in order to make it airtight. Fleet can send me the bill."

The man's face cracked a mischievous smile again. "Aye, sir."

***

Qin pulled Petty Officer Cullers off the engine cleanup detail and walked with him back toward the ship's main body. "Son, I've got a new task for you. The others can finish cleaning up."

Cullers wiped the sweat from his brow and focused on what Qin was about to say. His eyes were pale blue, and his hair matted brown.

"We're about to haul ass into the upper atmosphere of a gas giant. Pressure's going to be increased on the hull. We must shore up some areas to ensure we don't pop like a grape."

Cullers looked around, following Qin's eyes.

"I think this area is the weakest point in Engineering. I need you to do what you can to reinforce the accessways. We don't have much time to weld shut all the access panels and areas where you see thin hull plating. Understand?"

Cullers nodded, but his big eyes made it clear he was over his head.

"Don't worry, I'll help you. Now go break out the welder and meet me back here ASAP."

Cullers came to attention and then bolted back to Engineering. Qin eyed the walls of the narrow corridor suspiciously. He didn't relish the thought of this ship being his coffin.

***

There were five bodies on the deck when Lestor got to the corridor adjacent to the shuttle bay. Two were human and thus covered with sheets; the other three were dead Blue-Devils. Sergeant Rizzo stepped on the last body's arm as he approached her. He had no respect for the dead aliens.

"Ma'am, the shuttle's taken a few direct hits in the last firefight. You might want to see if she'll even move."

Lester nodded as she stepped around the bodies.

"Let's get these two crewmen removed. I don't want them anywhere near the aliens."

Rizzo looked down at the corpses. "What should we do with them?"

"Major Bray wanted to space that prisoner," Lestor said.

Rizzo nodded in agreement. "Space them, then?"

Lestor smiled deviously. She liked the way this guy thought.

"Space 'em."

Rizzo happily barked some orders and then followed Lestor into the shuttle bay. The burned metallic smell was nearly overpowering in the narrow bay. Another smell lingered, the sickening smell of death. Lestor swallowed hard and ignored the damaged walls, focusing instead on the Maser gun, still bolted to the deck. She cautiously approached it, wary of its raw power and radioactive death.

"Can you make the core meltdown on command?" she asked.

Rizzo approached the weapon as if it were an old friend. His gloved hand caressed the giant barrel. "The designers knew they had a weapon that could easily be converted into a bomb. So they made it a feature."

Lestor's face reflected her horror from behind the faceplate of her helmet.

"Don't worry, ma'am. It's not going to go off until we want it to."

Her obvious disgust with the weapon remained as she motioned to the shuttle. "Can you tap into the gun's system with the shuttle's computer?"

Rizzo ducked under the cannon's barrel and opened a panel on the side of the weapon. There were several standard data ports inside. "All you need is a shielded cable. There's no wireless capability."

"Okay, the data ports on the shuttle are along the center of the ceiling. Get this thing inside and hook it up. I'll write a routine to access it. Can you send me the service manual for the weapon?"

Rizzo nodded curtly.

She turned around and headed into the shuttle. The ragged metal from its sustained damage remained, a poignant reminder of another casualty. She sat down at the pilot controls and started assessing the damaged drive. The shuttle could not maintain a straight-line course, but she could keep it from falling by using the lifters. That would have to do. There wasn't time to reroute the starboard drive.

Chapter 15

Lieutenant Boxer scanned the immediate area again for Blue-Devils. Her search came back empty. There was nothing out there but chunks of ice and rock. The radiation detector startled no one as it went off. They needed to leave the ring; there was no time left to linger. Boxer silenced the alarm.

"Captain, the radiation has exceeded safe levels. We're starting to cook out here."

Xander sat in his chair, feet crossed and back stiff. He relaxed and sat up, punching the intercom. "Attention the ship, this is the Captain. Make preparations to depart. I repeat, make preparations for departure."

He turned to Boxer. "Get Vance and Lestor up on the double."

"Aye, sir."

***

Vance was in the enlisted head when the captain's announcement came. He quickly finished shaving and put on his gray uniform shirt, tucking it in and checking his gig line like he's done every day of his military career. They might be in a state of war, but he'd be damned if he was going to be anything but regulation in appearance. He was out in the main corridor when

Boxer's page found him. He answered it and told her he was on his way.

He met Lestor at the stairs to the upper deck. She was still in her spacesuit and carrying her helmet. Her short black hair was matted with sweat, and her face was still without makeup. Vance shook his head as she turned to see him.

"Hey, where's the cadet parade?" she asked.

Vance ignored the joke and followed her up the stairs.

"Don't get too close. My funk is fatal," she said.

"You're fine. Thanks for clearing out my cabin. Otherwise, I'd have nothing to wear."

She waited for him to climb up after her. He looked closely at her big, dark eyes and realized she was starting to look weary. Hopefully, this would all be over soon, and they could get much-needed rest on their way home.

"Are the shuttle and weapon ready to drop?"

Lestor nodded with effort. "She won't fly straight, but she'll drop as slow as we want. The gun's wired into the shuttle's control. We can initiate a meltdown on command."

Vance was honestly impressed. He patted her back in approval. "Nice job, Lieutenant. Let's go tell the Captain," he said, motioning for her to enter the bridge hatch he cracked open. She was too tired to smile, but he could tell she appreciated his gesture.

Lestor and Vance stood before Captain Xander, waiting for them near his chair.

"Number One, what's our status?"

Vance took a breath and then dove in. "Engineering is ready to give us full power. The forward deck breach has been secured and reinforced. Lieutenant Lestor has configured the nuke cannon to melt down on command. The shuttle is ready to drop it when we need it."

Xander raised a bushy gray eyebrow. He was not expecting so much work to be completed quickly. He noted how put together his first officer was and nearly said something, but another alarm thwarted his thoughts.

"Motion in the ring, sir. The alien ship is moving through the ice field," Boxer said incredulously.

Xander and Vance locked eyes. "I told you he's linear. The guy's obsessed with getting us. Okay, let's fire up the main and get moving."

Vance sat at the scanning station while Lestor plopped herself down hard at the helm.

"Engineering, full power," Xander said.

Qin's voice responded immediately. "Aye, sir. Full power."

"Continue forward with the ring before jetting for the planet. I want to see if he'll keep eating ice in pursuit," Xander directed.

"Aye, Captain."

The *Weippe* edged along the clearing away from the alien starship. Vance switched the main screen to a view aft. Sure enough, the huge orange ship plowed through the crushed ice and rock like an icebreaker ship, opening a path through a frozen river. Some smaller objects seemed to get vaporized by the shielding, but most were too big and were flung out of the way, creating endless chain reactions as they impacted other ring debris.

Captain Xander grinned like a fox. He loved it. Vance watched him laugh at the dogged determination of the alien captain.

"Ha, come and get us, you fool!"

Lestor calculated a new course and cued it on her screen. She kept looking up at the screen and shaking her tired head.

"Okay, Helm. Get us the hell out of here."

She punched in the course change, and the tiny ship altered its direction and headed away from the ring towards the swirling orange and white bands of the gas giant. "Coming to full speed. Estimated arrival time twenty-five minutes."

Xander's head turned aside as he registered the time.

"Shit, they'll be all over us by then."

Vance disagreed. "It will take them a few minutes to swing about in all that ice and rock. It'll slow them down a bit."

Xander pounded the intercom switch on his armrest. "Put the spurs to her, Qin!"

"She's at full gallop, Captain. No promises on whether she'll throw a shoe," Qin's craggy voice replied over the intercom.

Vance shook his head in disbelief at the old men and their rural humor. Coming from a farm in the hill country, he probably understood their language more than anyone else on the bridge. He just never expected anyone in the fleet to talk like farmhands.

The *Weippe* shuddered and seemed to lurch forward like an impatient cowboy boot urging her. The old hull creaked and cracked around them as they pulled clear of the ring and headed for the planet's billowy clouds.

Vance kept his eye on the stern cameras, trying to see if the alien ship was coming after them. His scans didn't indicate any immediate course change. He held his breath, hoping they took as long as possible to pursue them. Finally, after he started turning blue, the ship began altering its course. Instead of coming out of the ring in the most direct route, as the *Weippe* had done, it plowed through more ice and rock before turning wide, like an old cow. Vance chuckled to himself at the image in his mind. His father had an old cow named Merti, which they used to haul hay bales to the pasture. That ship turned like Merti with a full load behind her.

"They're finally coming about, sir."

Xander glanced at a secondary screen that showed the alien ship pulling free of the ice and gaining speed.

"Helm, be at the ready. We can't outrun them, but we sure can outturn the bastards," Xander said.

"Aye, sir."

Vance's instruments finally started estimating the speed of the vast, lumbering red-orange starship. It didn't look good. He swallowed hard and divulged the bad news. "They're gaining on us. Estimated intercept time in fifteen minutes."

Xander pounded his armrest again. "Helm, change course for the equatorial region. We don't have time to get to the pole."

"Aye, sir," Lestor said, scrambling to lay in the new course.

"Vance," Captain Xander asked.

"Calculating. Revised intercept time twenty minutes, sir."

Xander punched the intercom button hard. "Qin, you gotta give me more."

There was a lingering pause before the Engineer responded. His voice was calm and collected. Almost expectant.

"We're pushing the limit now. That's all she'll do, Captain."

Xander stood up fast, throwing his arms back as he rose, yelling, "Dammit, Qin!"

The ship bucked momentarily, sending the Captain to the floor headfirst. Vance could have sworn he felt a sudden increase in speed. Xander picked himself up off the floor and calmly sat as if nothing had happened.

Lestor and Vance exchanged puzzled looks.

"Revised intercept time?" Xander calmly asked.

"Nine minutes, sir."

Xander put a finger inside his wet collar and pulled it out.

"That's more like it."

They proceeded without comment for a while, everyone on the bridge wondering what they had just witnessed. Xander continued to watch the dual views fore and aft as the planet loomed large in front of them. Finally, he got up again and stood before Lestor's console. A quiet sigh left his lips before he spoke.

"How much maneuvering thrust do we have?"

"A few minutes, tops. I can't bleed the main until we reach the cloud level."

Xander licked his dry lips and thought for a moment.

"I want to make sure they follow us. Can you do a few corkscrews as we fall? I'd like to take some potshots at them. You know, let them know we care."

She grinned at the old man and nodded. "I think we can manage it, sir."

"Good. On my command," he said, returning to his seat.

"Weapons, we'll need a couple of well-placed shots into their faces. Navigation will barrel us over to give you several chances before we dive straight into the clouds."

"Aye, Captain," Boxer said. She started configuring the railgun turret to fire aft.

Vance kept his eyes on the enemy ship. It didn't look any different. It just kept getting larger by the minute.

Xander raised his right arm. "Ready to auger on my command."

"Ready, Captain."

Xander's excited eyes were locked on the view aft. He lowered his arm.

"Go!"

The Corvette's hull creaked again as the big gas giant spun around in the front view screens. A quarter of the way through the burn, the twin railguns fired several shots. They could almost feel the rounds re-chambering as the old ship turned.

Vance watched the alien starship's shields flash as the metallic rounds pierced them. He could see jets of gas escaping from the impact areas. It was probably internal air escaping from holes caused by the kinetic power from the impact.

"Hits across their bow. Probable hull breaches."

Xander pounded his armrest again, this time with satisfaction.

"Come get us, you blue bastards!"

As the *Weippe* corked around again, the main guns fired. The decks rumbled. Xander shouted, "Hold fire!"

"Helm, jigger our path a bit and counter-rotate. Before their targeting system can predict our position."

"Aye, Captain," Lestor said.

The ship twisted over again, this time in the opposite direction. Boxer recalculated the angle and fired again. There was a jolt that felt like the whole ship stuttered for a moment. The guns didn't fire.

"Jam on the number two barrel. Gun crew, clear the jam!" Boxer called into the intercom.

Xander looked back at the rear screen. The alien starship's head was glowing.

"Hang on, everyone, they're firing!" Xander hollered.

Chapter 16

Qin and the rest of his stokers were strapped into their seats, bracing for impact. They would never know if the Blue-Devils managed to hit the drive funnel. They'd all be dead, and the ship would careen into the gas giant like a flaming meteorite. Seen from aft, there was not much of a target to aim for that wasn't the drive. Like many other fleet vessels, the Corvette class starship was long and narrow. A few meters of metal girders hung to the starboard and port sides, but most of the ship's rear was funneled for the tunnel drive.

Seconds ticked by on the old analog watch he wore on his arm. Qin closed his eyes and said a prayer for the ship and himself. But nothing happened. He opened one eye and then the other. No plumes of radioactive plasma heading at him, just the same dirty white walls with chipped paint along the edges.

He glanced over at Petty Officer Cullers. The kid was looking back at him with big eyes. He probably wondered the same thing as Qin. Why weren't they dead?

The nearest porthole was behind a wall, and Qin could not look out. He punched up the stern camera and saw a swirling ring of ice but no enemy ship.

"Engineering to Bridge, what happened?"

Captain Xander's voice replied, "Rail gun's jammed. We're still trying to get into the stratosphere."

Qin shook his head. "I thought they fired at us."

"They did, old friend, and we successfully evaded. Thanks to our capable Helm."

Qin smiled. He always liked her better than anyone else on the ship.

"Way to pull the reins, Lieutenant."

Lestor's curt voice responded. "Thank you, sir."

"Engineering out," Qin said, knowing he shouldn't distract them any more than he already had.

"Sir, the inducer's beginning to overheat!" Cullers shouted.

Qin checked the temperature and made some adjustments to his panel.

"Okay, Cullers. Back her off a bit. See if that calms her."

Cullers ran his fingers over his controls, and they watched the temperature gauge hold steady. "Come on, baby, don't get all lathered up on me," Qin coaxed. The engine was going to be a horse to him from now on.

The gauges still didn't budge.

"Drop her off another notch."

"Aye, sir."

Qin tapped the glass panel as if that would somehow affect the temperature. It didn't, but it made him feel better. After giving it a minute longer, he resigned to the fact that it was not getting cooler. It got hotter by a degree.

"I don't think that's working, sir."

Qin flashed the kid an evil eye, and he looked back at his panel.

"Bridge, Engineering. We're starting to overheat. She's worked herself into a terrible lather."

"Dammit, Qin. I need a few minutes longer."

Qin shook his head. Don't you always? He cut off the intercom.

"I'm backing her off, Cullers. Initiate pressure release on my signal."

"Aye, sir."

Qin watched the schematic change on his screens and followed the steps in the checklist that he knew by heart. Slowly, the temperature fell back into an acceptable range.

"Engineering, Helm. Velocity bleeding off."

"If I don't ease her back, she'll overheat and melt down. You still have about eighty-five percent."

The intercom sputtered.

Qin and Cullers both looked at the speaker grill between them. It was silent. The ambient noise in the room dropped a few decibels as the drive adjusted to the new power setting. They looked at each other for a moment. Finally, Qin said, "I don't think they're talking to us anymore."

Qin started to laugh, and Cullers looked back at his schematics.

***

Lieutenant Boxer leaned over her intercom and pressed the button. "Sergeant, what's the hold-up?"

Rizzo answered immediately. "The number two barrel is jammed. We're still working to clear it."

Boxer's voice was as low as she could manage. "Hurry, mister."

"Wilco, out."

Vance was watching Boxer, and she knew it. She turned to him with a fake smile. "We should have weapons any minute now."

Vance nodded slowly and returned to his scans. The enemy ship was noticeably larger. Glowing circles of light appeared on both sides of the bow, and the energy signature blossomed in the infrared.

"They're powering up their weapons. Massive energy readings."

Captain Xander glanced back at Vance. "We're eight minutes away from the troposphere."

Vance shook his head. "If you have any trick plays, sir. Now's a good time to run them."

Xander returned his attention to the main screen. He stroked his gray beard a few times in thought. Then he punched the intercom. "Qin, I need to vent. Just like at Plaue. Remember?"

"I remember, Captain. Just give the word," Qin answered.

Xander exited his chair and walked over to Lestor, motioning for Vance to join them.

"Do we still have those alien bodies?"

"Aye, sir. I was going to have them ejected," Lestor replied.

"Put them in the starboard airlock. Vance, have them put every scrap piece of metal in that airlock. Then stand by there to blow it on my command."

Vance nodded curtly and headed out the hatch. As he skipped down the stairs, he grabbed the first rating he saw and had her come with him to the port side, where repairs had been made. There was plenty of debris left over, stacked in piles along the deck. "Grab some help and get all this junk into the starboard airlock ASAP."

"Aye, sir," she said, scrambling to get help.

Vance went through the area that had been sickbay, which now served as a temporary morgue. The two enlisted bodies were on the floor, and Torven's body was still on the bed, zipped into a black body bag. He had a decision to make. Use the human bodies or try to take them home. Whenever possible, it was regulated to return a body for proper burial. The only exceptions were when the safety of the rest of the crew was in jeopardy or when the fleet was at war. Deep space burial was the norm for exploration ships far from the Federation.

Cook Odem came by in the corridor, and Vance stopped him.

"Captain's ordered us to eject the dead. Have these bodies taken to the starboard airlock, fast!"

Odem seemed taken aback. He hesitated. "But, sir, they haven't had their last rites yet."

Vance got a few inches from the man's face. "If we don't do this, we'll be next. Understand?"

Odem slowly bobbed his head, perturbed by the request. He hollered down to the galley, and another man came to help him move the bodies.

"Where are the dead aliens?" Vance asked.

Odem shrugged. "Already in the airlock, sir."

Great, no wonder he thinks I'm nuts. Vance led the way to the airlock, grabbing another rating to help him open the hatch. He supervised the loading of the bodies and then the scraps of metal and plastic left over from the repairs. It didn't look like much, but it would have to do.

"Bridge, airlock two is ready."

Captain Xander replied. "Excellent. Stand by to release."

The ship was still rotating, and Vance could hear the retros firing as its course changed.

"Brace for impact!" the Captain exclaimed over the ship's intercom.

Vance and everyone else in the corridor were tossed onto their butts by a tremendous impact on the hull. It felt like the entire ship was face-slapped by a giant hand. Vance scrambled back to his feet to man the airlock release button. Everyone else got to their feet and headed back to their duty stations.

"Engineering, vent! Lieutenant Vance, eject the debris!"

Vance pushed the button and swore he felt the pressure pull as everything in the airlock was sucked out into space. He watched it go from a nearby porthole. Glittering bits of metal jutted out from the ship in a steady stream. It was kind of beautiful and dreadful at the same time. He could see the massive, swirling clouds on the horizon as they continued to dive for the planet.

"Engineering, bridge. Please respond," the Captain's voice came over the ship's PA.

Vance started for Engineering, sensing something was wrong. As he got to the access tube, he peered out of a square porthole at the mess that was the stern section of the ship. Whatever had hit them, Engineering took the brunt of it. The only good thing he saw was that it was still there.

He punched the intercom. "Bridge, Vance. I'm at the stern access tube. I can see all kinds of damage to Engineering from here."

"Emergency crew to Engineering. Vance, get back there and see what's going on!" the Captain ordered.

Vance started unlocking the hatch and removing the extra seals the crew had just added. When he was done, two ratings—a young woman and Cook Odem — joined him with first aid bags.

"Odem, get a radiation reading before we enter," Vance said.

Odem pulled out a handheld instrument and waved it around. It clicked and sputtered until it finally gave him a reading. "It's higher than the rest of the ship but passable."

Vance nodded and then took the lead down the tube. They had to go through more sealed hatches before entering Engineering, so gaining access took longer than usual.

Vance motioned for another radiation check. Odem held up his detector and frowned. "Make it quick, sir; the levels are much higher here."

Vance took the detector and told the others to wait for him. Odem and the woman stayed behind, looking worried.

Holding the detector before him, Vance carefully rounded the corner to Engineering. The room was eerily quiet, and flashing radiation warning lights blinked like strobes. He moved over to the emergency panel and opened it. Inside, he found an oxygen mask and a portable tank. He took a moment to strap the mask on and then activated it. Hearing nothing but his breathing, he continued through the entrance to the main reactor.

Steam poured through a grill on the wall and billowed overhead like white, puffy clouds. He saw someone's legs lying on the floor and came closer to examine them. It was Petty Officer Cullers. He was unconscious and barely breathing. Vance pulled him over his shoulders and carried him out of the room and back to where the others were waiting. Odem took the man from Vance and set him gently down. The woman immediately started checking his vitals.

"Come with me, grab a breather for yourself," Vance said, catching his breath. The two of them ran back into Engineering to search for the others.

As Odem strapped on his mask, Vance held up three fingers. "There should be three more in here, including Commander Qin."

Odem nodded and followed Vance into the steam-filled reactor room. They moved through the steam, keeping low to find people better. It didn't take them long to find two more bodies lying prone on the deck. Each man struggled to get a person over his shoulders and stumbled back to the entrance.

The woman helped get the crewmen to the ground and immediately started tending to them. One young woman had a gash on her forehead that was still bleeding, and the man Vance carried was utterly still. It took the medic no time to determine he was dead. She returned to dressing the woman's wound with materials in her med bag.

"Come on, we still have to find Qin," Vance said, pulling Odem back.

The reactor room was hot and humid. Odem and Vance's uniforms were completely soaked with sweat. Vance had them get down on all fours and crawl around the circular room, looking for Qin. Starting from opposite directions, they soon met on the other side, shaking their heads—no Qin.

"Is there anywhere else to check?" Vance asked.

"I've never even been in here before, sir."

Vance tried to think back to the ship's blueprints he had studied on the trip out to the rim. It seemed like there were maintenance anti-chambers that led around the funnel. He went where he thought they'd be and felt around the wall until he found a hatch.

"On the other side, there should be another of these chambers. Go and see if Qin is in it. I'll check this one."

Odem nodded, gave the thumbs-up sign, and then scurried away into the mist. Vance proceeded inside the narrow chamber. One lone light was at the far end, and he could see a silhouetted figure. It was Qin. He was attempting to repair a pipe. Vance approached, and Qin was startled to see him.

"Are you okay, sir?"

Qin nodded and motioned for Vance to help him tighten the fitting on the pipe. "We have to secure this so the main doesn't overheat."

Vance and Qin struggled to turn the fitting another quarter turn before Qin held up his hand to stop.

"Let's get out of here and let it vent," Qin said. His breath labored from struggling with the pipe.

Odem met them back in Engineering. The condensation clouds lifted as they hurried back to where the others were.

Qin looked around at the wounded and sat beside Petty Officer Cullers. The young spacer was awake and looked up at him. "Is the main secured, sir?"

"Yes, for now. Thanks for your help, son. That last shot almost doomed us."

Cullers looked over at Vance, who had joined them, taking a knee.

"What's our status, Commander?"

Qin sighed and looked back at the entrance to Engineering.

"I'd say we just got our butts kicked," Qin said. Vance wasn't looking for commentary, and Qin knew it.

"Not sure what the funnel looks like, but the shielding on the stern saved us from that last shot. Gonna need repairs before we can tunnel again," Qin said, looking around at his staff lying on the floor. "If you can spare some bodies, we can work on it."

Vance nodded. "I'll see what I can do." He looked down at Cullers and touched his shoulder. "Nice work, Petty Officer."

The kid smiled weakly in return.

Chapter 17

Vance entered the bridge and went to Captain Xander's side. The room was bathed in orange light, as if cruising into a sunset. The bilious clouds of the gas giant planet were outside the portholes and on the monitors. The stern camera had been damaged during the last attack, its signal shorted but still able to show the lumbering alien starship moving through the clouds like a giant whale.

"Engineering took the brunt of the last hit. Commander Qin has requested extra bodies to begin his repairs," Vance started.

Xander nodded, and Vance could see the troubled look on his old face.

"How's Qin look?"

"He's okay, sir. A bit shaken but physically fine."

Xander eased his worried look. Then he changed the topic. "Can we proceed with the drop?"

Vance eyed Lestor, who was still in her spacesuit at her post. She slowly nodded, her expression grim. He looked over at Boxer, who also dipped her head.

"I think we're ready, Captain."

Xander stared up at the forward monitor. Vance waited for the order to descend, but the Captain said nothing. He just stared hard at the swirling storm clouds.

The ship was weathering the wind gusts at this altitude despite being designed for space, not planetary atmospheres.

"Take us down, First Officer," Xander finally said.

Vance glanced at Lestor. "Helm, begin the descent."

"Aye, sir. Descending 100 meters per second."

The *Weippe* nosed down, and the old hull released a single, rumbling creak of protest. Vance wrapped his fingers around a handhold in case it got rougher. Lestor sat down at her station and strapped in. The sound of others on the bridge clicking their seat belts echoed off the walls. Xander eventually did the same in his captain's chair.

"Approaching the planet's troposphere," Lestor said.

Everyone's eyes were drawn to the primary monitor. The ship dipped below the orange haze and fell into a vast cavern of clouds with layers of orange, red, and white colors. They felt like they were descending into a colorful, impossibly deep, wide canyon.

"It's… beautiful," Lestor said aloud.

Xander pointed to the nearest wall of clouds. "Helm, get us over there inside the clouds. We're trying not to be seen."

Lestor complied, edging the *Weippe* on thrusters while continuing their descent.

Vance kept his eyes on the atmospheric pressure gauges. They were falling fast and approaching 1 bar, about Selene sea level. As soon as the ship entered the colorful clouds, they could feel the fierce winds pushing them along like a bird in a gale.

Xander switched to the stern camera in time to see the burned-orange alien ship fade out behind the darker clouds. Vance switched to scanner mode, and an outline of the alien ship appeared in the dark clouds. They were still in pursuit and staying at the *Weippe.*

"Okay, Helm, let's see if they are serious about chasing us," Xander said.

"Aye, sir. Descending to two bars," Lestor replied.

The ship's hull began to creak like an old-time diving bell. Scattered shots could be heard all around them. Rivets popped in the decks below, but the Corvette hull held.

"Easy, Helm. We can't afford a rupture. Slow and steady," Xander urged.

Vance kept his eyes on the altimeter. As they sank, the pressure outside far eclipsed the everyday pressures of normal planets. The ship was not designed to dive into atmospheres like submarines diving into water. The atmospheres of gas giants were dens, and descending into them was every bit like descending deep into the oceans of rocky planets. There was a point where the Corvette hull would not be able to withstand any more outside pressure, and it would crush. The problem was that nobody knew what the crush depth was. All they could do was guess based on mathematical formulas never designed for use with a starship.

The *Weippe* jolted, and everyone grabbed something to keep upright. Their forward momentum was suddenly altered in a lateral motion as the ship creaked again, much louder than before.

"Level out here, Helm," Xander said.

The ship continued to shudder. More rivets popped, this time on the bridge. The screaming projectiles missed the humans but nailed the secondary monitor, cracking it.

Xander lifted a bushy gray eyebrow and turned to Vance. "Let's get the shuttle launched."

"Aye, sir."

Vance took Lestor's spot as she slid over to the Engineering station, where she had arranged the controls to steer the shuttle remotely. She removed her suit gloves to get a better feel for the touch screens.

"Powering up the *Ericson*," she said.

Lieutenant Boxer changed her screen to display the remote controls for the Army cannon. She waited for Lestor to launch before proceeding to arm the weapon.

"Engineering, bridge. Standby to cut the main," Xander said over the ship's intercom.

"Engineering, aye."

It was not Qin's voice but rather Petty Officer Cullers. Xander glanced at Vance but said nothing. Vance frowned and tilted his head in confusion. The Commander might be busy with his new stokers and put Cullers in charge. Vance could tell his captain was nervous, but not enough to say anything. Xander slowly returned his attention to the main screen.

The orange and white clouds had given way to dark, almost red clouds as the Jovian atmosphere thickened around them.

"Do we still have them on the scopes?"

Boxer opened another screen and brought up Vance's controls. After a quick study, she replied, "Aye, sir. They are one hundred and five meters off our stern."

Boxer threw up a graphic on the edge of the primary monitor. It showed the alien ship as a white vector drawing with a range of target numbers underneath it. Xander focused on the graphic. "Come on, you Blue-Devils. You know we're still here, come and get us."

The bridge was lit up by a flash of lightning so bright it caused everyone's eyes to see spots. Superbolts of lightning were standard in the atmospheres of gas-giant planets, but that didn't stop everyone from thinking they were under attack again.

"Confirmed, electrostatic discharge, not weapons fire," Boxer stated for everyone's benefit.

Lestor struggled with control of the *Ericson* as another bolt of lightning scrambled her signal. "This is not going to be easy with all this electricity frying the air," she said aloud.

"Do your best, Lieutenant," Vance urged her.

Lestor nodded as she repeated her steps to launch the shuttle. Moments later, she reported her progress. "*Ericson* is underway and falling steady."

"Activate the gun," Vance ordered.

"Gun overload initiated."

Xander clicked the intercom. "Engineering, cut power now."

"Aye, Captain. Main is offline, reactor shutting down," Cullers responded.

The background sounds of the bridge, air circulation fans, and equipment cooling fans fell silent. The lights dimmed to just a few red emergency lights running off batteries.

"Let's hope there's no history of naval warfare where they come from," Xander muttered.

A camera was on top of the shuttle, and Lestor put the image in the left corner of the primary monitor. It showed the *Weippe* receding quickly, disappearing in the dark red clouds. Lestor angled the view to the stern of the shuttle, hoping to pick up the enemy ship tracking behind it. There were too many dark clouds, and the shuttle fell at the same rate as the Corvette.

The range numbers on the alien ship's graphic started to change. It was getting farther away from the *Weippe*.

"They've taken the bait," Xander said, delight in his raised voice.

"Affirmative, Captain. The alien ship is continuing to pursue the *Ericson*," Boxer said.

Xander let out a hoot of delight, startling Vance. He'd never seen the old man react so boldly to anything. This brought a smile to his face as he looked over to Lestor. She was grinning too. The plan was working almost perfectly.

Another bolt of lightning flashed outside the *Erickson*, revealing the macabre shape of the orange enemy starship.

"Helm, steer us up."

"Aye, sir," Lestor replied.

"Let's see how far she'll follow. That hull of hers looks twice as thick as our hide," Xander said. Vance could tell he was enjoying the ruse now that it was working.

"Sir, they've slowed their pursuit," Boxer said.

Xander looked back at Vance, a slight panic in his old eyes again.

"How many bars are on the shuttle?"

Before Lestor could answer, the shuttle imploded, and all signals were lost. "Nearly three bars before the pressure crushed it."

"Reading a small nuclear explosion from the *Ericson's* position," Boxer stated. Data and images streamed on the primary monitor, showing the mushroom cloud swirling apart in the high Jovian winds. The *Weippe* shuddered as the shock wave passed through them.

Xander pointed to the alien ship on the screen. "What about them?"

"Too much static," Boxer said, focusing on her instruments.

A few seconds passed that seemed to Vance like an eternity. It was starting to get noticeably warm on the bridge, and with the power cut to a minimum, sweat was forming on everyone's brows. He kept scanning his screens and then looking up at the main viewer. Finally, the image of the alien ship focused through the clouds. She was unscathed and rising towards them.

"Helm, roll us over. Lay into them with everything we have," Xander shouted.

The *Weippe* slowly rolled over, and the ship's gravity held, keeping everyone on their feet. Vance unstrapped and moved to Boxer's side. He pointed to the spot on the enemy vessel where he thought they were weakest. Above them, it was near their stern, in a section with five large circular constructs. He was betting they were vents for their drives. He moved his fingers towards the large, black tubes that were presumably drives.

"Lay your fire across there," he said.

She nodded in agreement with him and laid in the coordinates. "Firing solution set, commencing the attack," she told the Captain.

The *Weippe* recoiled as the massive railgun fired a steady stream of metal darts tipped with depleted uranium. Boxer slid the view below them up on the main viewer so everyone could see the results.

The ship fell silent as the guns stopped as suddenly as they had begun.

"Engineering, we need the main lit ASAP!" Captain Xander shouted into the intercom.

"Already coming up now, Captain. Ready in thirty seconds," came the tired voice of Qin.

Xander smiled as he made eye contact with Vance.

"Thanks, old friend."

The *Weippe* answered by coming alive, with lights brightening and air circulation vents pumping again. Vance glanced back at Lester, who allowed a slight grin as she wiped her forehead and prepared a course heading.

Boxer studied her gun cameras as the enemy ship started leaking gases and tilted over as if sinking. "I think they're going down!" she exclaimed aloud.

Everyone on the bridge gave a cheer cut short by a sudden jolt that sent Vance flying into the nearest wall. He slid to the floor and started scrambling back to a seat.

"What the hell was that?" Xander demanded.

Boxer adjusted her instruments. "Some kind of force field from the enemy ship. They're pulling us down with them!"

Xander punched the intercom hard with the palm of his hand. "Engineering, give us all you've got. We're going to pull away."

"Copy," Qin responded.

The *Weippe* started sinking fast, pulled under like a tethered fisherman who had hooked a whale. Everyone grabbed their stations for support; it felt like they were riding an express elevator straight down.

"Main red-lined, Captain. That's all she'll do."

Xander implored Boxer, who ignored him and focused on her instruments.

"Take another shot at the focus point of that field," Vance suggested as he slid into his seat and strapped in.

"I'm all out of rails," Boxer exclaimed. Her dark eyes focused on Vance.

"Helm, angle down, and roll us like a stuck fish!" Xander shouted.

Vance looked over at the Captain. His steel eyes were wide open as if he were mad. Lestor seemed afraid to do anything. Her hands paused, shaking above her controls.

"Push hard against their beam. We might be able to break it. But it'll mean we go deeper," Vance stated.

Xander nodded slowly. "It's all we have; do it or die anyway."

"Agreed, sir," Vance said.

Lestor's fingers resumed their dance over her instruments, and the ship lurched as they rolled back over and dove. The hull creaked again, louder than before and with more urgency. Vance watched several rivets burst, sending metal projectiles across the bridge like bullets. Xander never once flinched, like some ancient cavalryman leading a charge through a hail of lead.

The *Weippe* pushed under the enemy vessel at its stern, where she had no weapons they had noticed. As soon as they passed lower than the enormous black drive funnels, a single energy shot erupted from an unseen weapon barrel just under the drives.

The shot passed through the trestles holding the stern engine section to the *Weippe's* main body. One of the beams was cut off clean, but the ship stayed intact as it passed under the burned orange monster.

Everyone lurched forward again as the force field was pinched. Lestor brought the nose of the Corvette upward immediately. They held on as the ship rose through the now gray and black clouds. Vance thought he had heard something sloshing against the hull and quickly realized it was probably liquid hydrogen. They were far lower than anyone had dared to fall. He looked at the old gray walls of the ship and imagined them bursting at any moment, but nothing happened.

A huge shock wave pushed them forward as they climbed.

"Enemy ship destroyed!" Vance reported, not believing his own crudely working instruments that recorded the explosion.

Nobody cheered because they were convinced they would be next to implode, but the *Weippe's* hull remained intact as they rose into the higher levels of the planet's atmosphere.

"Helm, reduce speed to escape velocity," Xander said.

"Aye, sir."

Vance pulled a handheld fire extinguisher under his console and doused the electrical fire with white retardant. Sweat dribbled into his eyes, and he wiped it away with a sleeve. The ship smelled of burned electrical relays and human body odor. He let out a long sigh as he surveyed the bridge. The crew was still tense, but Vance could tell everyone was starting to relax the closer they got to space. *We won!*

Chapter 18

The damage control reports began streaming in before the *Weippe* made orbit. Vance's screens were flooded with requests for help from all areas of the ship. The pressure damaged two decks, leaking precious oxygen into the void. Electrical fires were reported from stem to stern. Vance got on his headset and started issuing orders for the repairs, prioritizing on the fly.

"Bridge, this is Sergeant Rizzo."

The call came over the ship's PA from the weary Surface Army NCO.

"Go ahead," Vance replied from his station.

"Sir, we got a problem. The starboard upper support beam has been completely sheared off," Rizzo stated, his voice an even strain.

Vance looked up at the Captain, who had stepped off his chair to stretch.

"We can't tunnel without it," Vance stated.

Xander's graying beard hid his face in the dim light of the bridge as he moved into a pool of white light near Vance's station. The first officer could see the concern in his captain's gray eyes. They had to make more than one tunnel jump to get home. They were stuck here if the ship couldn't make a single jump for structural reasons.

"We don't have anything strong enough to repair that beam," Vance said, his voice barely audible.

"Ask him how long a piece he needs," Xander said.

"Rizzo, this is Vance. How much beam is gone?"

There was a long pause as everyone waited for Rizzo's response.

Finally, his voice came through clear and strong over the PA. "At least six meters."

Vance and Xander shook their heads in disgust. There wasn't enough plasteel on the ship to replace that critical beam. Both men turned away in thought. Vance wiped his forehead with the back of his wet uniform sleeve. Xander moved slowly back to his chair, shoulders slumped.

"What about ripping metal from the damaged decks?" Lieutenant Boxer asked.

Xander shook his head. "Not thick enough."

In a moment of inspiration, Lestor ran some calculations on her screens. She stopped typing and looked over at Vance.

"What about the *Wayfinder*?"

Captain Xander slowly stroked his beard and turned in his chair to look at his First Officer. Vance started to smile. The *Wayfinder*. He had completely forgotten about it.

"The *Wayfinder* is a newer hull design. She's got to have stronger composites than we do. The only trouble will be cutting and placing them on the *Weippe*," Vance said.

"Helm, get us back to the *Wayfinder*. Lieutenant, get a crew together and start making plans to salvage whatever we need from the civilian ship. I don't want to linger out here. We don't know when more Blue-Devil ships will show."

"Aye, sir."

Before Vance could stand up, another voice crackled over the intercom. It was Odem, the cook. "Captain, you need to get to sickbay now."

"What is it, Odem?" Xander asked, sensing the urgency in the cook's tone.

"Commander Qin, sir."

Xander bolted out of his chair and headed for the exit hatch. Vance motioned to Boxer to follow him, and they left the bridge to Lestor.

***

The sickbay was still just a bed in a cramped space that used to be part of the ship's pantry. A crude medical diagnostic scanner was over the bed, with glowing monitors at the headboard. Odem stood over Commander Qin's body, closely watching his vitals and trying to make the man comfortable.

Captain Xander slowly approached his old friend, unsure of what was happening to him.

"Captain, he's suffering from extreme radiation exposure," Odem cautioned.

Odem was wearing a lead apron and held up his arms to stop Xander from getting closer. Xander's face was drained of color as he stopped short of coming to Qin's side. Odem backed away, took off his apron, and handed it to Xander.

"He's in and out, but I thought you should see him before he passes."

Xander put on the apron and nodded solemnly to Odem. The cook's lean face was drawn and sad. He had served with Qin and Xander for the past few years, which was as hard on him as the Captain.

Xander came to Qin's side and stared into the older man's peaceful, round face.

"Qin, can you hear me, old friend?"

Qin stirred, and his eyes twitched but didn't open. "Aye, Captain."

"I have to ask, is the main capable of a tunnel jump? We still have to get home."

Qin shook his head with great effort. "No. Cullers knows what needs to be done."

Xander put his hand on Qin's shoulder to calm him. "Is there anything we can use from the *Wayfinder*?"

Qin opened one eye and stared up at Xander. "Containment core," he gasped and was cut off by a coughing fit that shook his body.

Odem tapped Xander's shoulder and pulled him back away. He pulled the lead apron off the captain and returned to Qin's side as the medical scanner started redlining. Odem worked furiously for a few minutes to no avail. The chief engineer was gone. Odem pulled a blanket over his head and exited the room to where Xander stood.

"I'm sorry, sir. There wasn't anything more we could have done for him."

Xander nodded and grabbed Odem's arm for reassurance. "Thank you for calling me, Seif."

Odem lowered his eyes and whispered a prayer in his native tongue. Xander bowed his head and said farewell to his old friend. Then he moved down the narrow corridor and punched an intercom button.

"Engineering, this is the Captain."

"Go, Captain," Cullers responded.

"Qin is dead, son. You're in command back there. What's your status?"

There was a pause as Cullers absorbed the news. Then he responded with more assurance than Xander would have guessed. "Sir, we barely have containment. The radiation is under control, but we can't make a tunnel until I can get at least eighty percent containment."

"We're heading back to the hull of the *Wayfinder*. Can you make use of their containment fields?"

Xander released the intercom button and waited. He knew the young man's head was spinning, so he waited patiently for a response. "Yes, Captain. I believe we can."

"Good. Lieutenant Vance is putting together a team to recover some hull beams. Get with him and organize a boarding party to retrieve whatever you need from the *Wayfinder*."

"Aye, sir."

"And son, Commander Qin had complete faith in you, so I won't question whatever you need. Is that clear? Do what you must, and I will see you get the help you need. Our lives depend on making at least one jump back to known space."

Culler's voice was more timid in responding. "Thank you, sir. We won't let you down."

Xander released the intercom button and tried to clear his head. Then, he activated the intercom again. "Captain to bridge."

"Helm here, Captain," Lestor responded.

"Lestor, hand off the helm and get to Engineering. Chief Cullers needs all the support we can give him."

"Aye, sir. On my way."

Odem shuffled down the hall and stopped before Xander.

"Captain, I need to get Qin's body off the ship. He's too hot."

Xander sighed. He didn't want to leave his friend behind, but he'd already consigned several other crewmen to space. "Get him into the airlock and jettison him. Let me know when you're ready, and I'll say a few words."

Odem wore a sad smile. "He would have wanted a burial in space, Captain. He was just an old space dog at heart. If you don't mind my saying, sir."

"I agree, Seif. I completely agree."

***

The *Weippe* cruised to the last known location of the *Wayfinder* before slowing down and heaving as close as possible. Captain Xander was back on the bridge to oversee the parking maneuver. He tried not to hover over the Helm, knowing that the NCO replacing Lestor was probably not an experienced driver. Very early on in his command career, he learned when to trust someone with a task and when to keep a close eye on them.

"Keep us in tight, but not so tight we scrape paint," Xander reiterated.

"Aye, Captain."

Xander went to the porthole and eyeballed the *Wayfinder*. She looked like a savanna carcass, after the predators had consumed the meaty bits. She was covered with black scorch marks across her side and burned holes through her hull like a hot steel rod rammed through flesh. It was difficult for an old spacer like himself to see a starship trashed that badly.

Xander walked back to his chair and clicked the PA. "You're clear to launch, Lieutenant."

"Aye, sir, launching," replied Vance.

Looking around the bridge, Xander realized he was the only officer left on deck. It was full of kids attempting to retrieve parts from a dead ship without a shuttle. Madness. He returned to the porthole and waited until he could make out four silver spacesuits tethered together and to the *Weippe*, zipping along on handheld rocket thrusters. Lieutenant Vance and Sergeant Rizzo were heading to the nearest structural beam, and Lieutenant Lestor and Cullers were heading sternward to what remained of the *Wayfinder's* mains.

Xander looked back towards the Scanning console. A young woman was sitting where Boxer usually sat, trying to make sense of the controls.

"Anything on the long-range set, Petty Officer Hines?"

She looked up with a blank stare on her round, youthful face. "Nothing, sir."

"Keep scanning. I don't want to be caught with half my staff stuck in the black."

"Aye, sir."

Xander looked at his reflection in the thick glass of the porthole. His bearded face was tired and drawn. He was running on emergency rations and mild stimulants. The coffee was bitter and strong, though, as he liked it. He couldn't remember when he or anyone else had slept longer than a five-minute nap. Coffee would be good about now. *Where the hell is my yeoman?* He looked back at the bridge crew and realized the yeoman was running Vance's station. Hell, I'm going to have to get my damn coffee.

He strolled over to the coffee station and assessed the damage. There was no water, only a few grounds in the bin, and no disposable cups. So much for that.

Chapter 19

Rizzo was in the lead and reached the nearest structural beam first. He circled the massive square beam with his metallic rope and secured himself to the *Wayfinder*. Before heading over, they had studied the blueprints of the ship. It was a standard starship construction consisting of three component sections, all held together by four structural beams. Engineers left off the skin around these areas to reduce weight and make repairs to vital components easier.

The beams were made from four sections of plasteel, each about five meters long, held together by seam rivets and composite layers. Removing the sections they needed would probably take them eight hours. With only hand tools and limited manpower, the job was far more significant than anyone cared to consider. Vance secured himself to the same beam just a bit further than the structural break to give himself space to work.

He looked up and saw Rizzo lighting his torch and getting to business. *This is not what I imagined myself doing in the Fleet. My damn grandfather was a welder, not me. I'm supposed to be the educated one.* He glanced around at the nearby gas giant that had nearly crushed them and at the battered old Corvette that had somehow survived. Life could be worse, he decided as he lit his torch.

***

Lieutenant Lestor hovered safely at a distance as Petty Officer Cullers wedged himself between pipes and fittings to reach the containment field covers he was after. She could smell the funk inside her spacesuit, making her want to cry. Her skin was oily and dirty, and her hair was beyond being human anymore. At least not a civilized human. She just wanted to get out of her suit and into a warm shower. She was tired, too, but that didn't bother her as much as suffocating in her body odor.

"Can you reach them?" She asked over the suit comm.

"I think so, ma'am. Though I'm not sure how we'll get them out."

Lestor assessed the various plasma cutters she had tied to her waist.

"I reckon we have enough tools to cut through anything in our way."

There was silence for a moment, and all Lestor could hear was her breathing inside the suit. Then, the comm crackled.

"Only one of the three containment field covers is usable, ma'am. And it's the one furthest away and buried the deepest," Cullers said.

"Figures."

***

Several hours later, the senior staff was back in the wardroom for the first time since the deck had been breached. Three of them were missing, and their empty chairs unnerved everyone there. Captain Xander began by addressing their absent crewmates.

"As most of you have no doubt learned by now, we have lost Commander Qin. Along with Major Bray and Lieutenant Torven, we have also lost five enlisted crewmen. Let's take a moment to acknowledge our friends and fellow warriors who have made the ultimate sacrifice."

Everyone bowed their heads in silence. Xander was not particularly religious, and he offered no prayer. When a minute had passed, he looked up and said, "We still have much work to do before we can get home. I realize that most of you and the crew are running on frayed nerves and little sleep. We're returning to Condition Yellow, and I expect everyone to break into shifts and get some rest. If we can't make at least two jumps back to Federation space, we could be stranded for a long time.

"Comm silence is still in effect. I'm not anticipating more Blue Devil ships, but we must assume they could arrive at any moment. Okay, progress reports on damage control. Go," he said to Vance.

"Rizzo and I managed to cut off the beam we needed. All we need to do now is remove the other end and haul it back over. I will need a couple of ratings in suits to help us graft it onto the *Weippe*."

Xander nodded, then he looked across at Lestor. She cleared her throat and started, "The containment field cover we needed was buried under all kinds of pipes and fittings we had to cut through. Cullers and I managed to get it off the *Wayfinder* and back to the *Weippe*. He thinks it won't take nearly as long to swap them once we get back to it. We're probably looking at another four to six hours of work to complete the swap."

"Excellent! Great work, Lieutenant. Put the Engineering team on shifts and let Cullers sleep first.

He's our best Engineer now, and I need him alert and rested."

Lestor sighed. "Aye, Captain."

Xander pointed to Boxer, who seemed surprised he picked her. Her eyes got big for a second. "What's the status of our defenses should the Devils return?"

"Ah, well. We're out of ammo for the main gun, and Engineering won't be able to shield us much until their repairs are made. Hull integrity held before, but there's no way we'd survive another go with one of their ships."

Xander shook his head as if he were upset. Boxer glanced at Vance, unsure what else to say.

"Is there anything aboard the *Wayfinder* that could be used as a weapon?" Vance asked.

Boxer curled her brow and looked at him incredulously. "Not that I can think of, sir."

"I'm asking because it was a science and exploration ship, not a military one. They might have an accelerator or some other instrument that could be made into a weapon."

Boxer shook her head slowly as she tried to recall the manifest of the *Wayfinder*. "I'll examine her records again with that in mind, sir."

Vance looked sharply back at Captain Xander.

"Can we use the metal from the *Wayfinder* to create more rods for the railgun to fire? That would be the first thing I'd look into," Vance said to Boxer.

"Aye, sir. Engineering uses the replication machinery. I might be able to fashion something from scrap metal."

"Do that first," Xander finished. Boxer nodded curtly.

Xander stood back up and looked down at his remaining senior staff.

"Let's meet back here in twenty-four hours for an update. That's all."

Everyone came to attention.

"Dismissed."

***

Vance tried to get Rizzo to take the second watch, but the man was insistent that he could wait. So Vance briefed him on what would happen next and assigned two other crewmen to help him. Then Vance dragged his tired ass back to his new bunk in Torven's cabin. He didn't even bother washing up, just stripped and climbed under the sheets, lights out in no time.

Seconds later, someone was poking him on the shoulder.

"Hey, get up, Lieutenant!"

It was a woman's voice, but didn't match the woman in his dream.

"Vance! Get up."

The poke became a shove.

"I'm awake," he groaned.

"The shower's free if you need it," Lestor urged.

She slipped back to her side, wearing a towel and carrying her shower bag. Vance slowly stretched his arms out wide to get his blood flowing. After a yawn, he grabbed his towel and bag and headed into the corridor. It was freezing cold, and he was well on his way before realizing he was naked. Crewmen passed with surprised smirks on their faces as he fumbled to cover himself with his towel.

Back in his cabin, he quickly dressed and headed for the galley. Rizzo was there by himself, and Cook Odem was frying something that looked like a sausage and smelled pretty good. Odem set a metal plate down in front of Vance, along with a cup of coffee.

"Thanks, Odem."

"Sausage and powdered eggs are coming up, sir," Odem said in his usual cheerful voice. Sausages were a regulation mystery meat that came in a tube of pig's gut. They usually tasted okay, fried up, but Odem added something to them to make them taste different depending on the meal. They usually got them straight for breakfast with a side of salt and pepper eggs to make them edible.

"How'd it go, Sarge?" Vance asked after a sip of coffee.

Rizzo looked just about dead. His uniform was sweaty, and his hair was matted with sweat. His normally black skin was matted with streaks of grease and dirt and wet with sweat.

"We got one side attached, sir. But the other one's going to give us a hard time. She's going to need trimming, and that takes time. I have the second kid you assigned to me working your shift. Should be along shortly, or else I'll have to drag his butt out of bed."

Vance chuckled. Rizzo sounded like a father of a teenager, and in many ways, he was. These enlisted kids were often just out of secondary school and wet behind the ears.

"Is he any good with a plasma cutter?"

Rizzo shrugged.

"Okay, man. Take a shower and get some sleep," Vance said.

Rizzo dragged himself up just as the young kid came, sniffing the sausages cooking.

"Have a seat, son; we'll be heading outside shortly to finish off the beam installation," Vance said to the freckled-faced kid as he took a bite of the red sausage.

"Name's Dawson, sir."

"Grab yourself some food, Dawson. Going to be a long day in the dark."

Chapter 20

Captain Xander was getting dressed in his cabin when a knock came at the hatch. He was wearing pants and had just put on his shirt, so he hollered for whoever it was to enter.

It was Lieutenant Boxer coming off her shift to report to him. Her shoulders were slumped, and her dark eyes were bloodshot from lack of sleep.

"End of shift report, Captain."

"Go ahead, Lieutenant, pardon my dressing."

She didn't seem to care about what he looked like. He motioned for her to sit on his bunk while he finished tucking his shirt in.

"The main beam is half installed. Sergeant Rizzo's crew did a fantastic job. Should be finished late into the next shift."

Xander nodded for her to continue, slipping his socks and shoes on next.

"Engineering has installed the new containment field cover. Lieutenant Lestor has doubts if it will work. She said she'd know for sure next shift when she and Cullers test the tunnel drive. We may only get one jump before the cover fails or something else."

She paused in thought and pounded her forehead with her palm. "There was something else, sir."

Xander nodded as he pulled on his service coat. He looked down at her and finally hiked a finger over his shoulder. "Get some rest, Boxer. Gonna be a long shift coming up."

She nodded, "Thanks, Captain."

"Oh yeah, there are some odd readings on the long-range scans. I think Lieutenant Vance should investigate them."

"I'll have him look into them." He opened the hatch, and she pulled herself up and headed out into the corridor like a zombie. Xander strapped on his service revolver and headed down the corridor towards Engineering.

The image of Qin dying stuck in his mind as he walked into the galley. Odem was there and shoved a cup of coffee into his hands as he passed, like some race car on pit row. "I'll be back for some breakfast," Xander said over his shoulder as he continued to Engineering.

"Better hurry, sir; the sausages are going fast."

Xander waved back at him as he entered another narrow corridor.

***

Engineering was hot and humid, and everyone there was covered in sweat and grease. Petty Officer Cullers approached the captain. "Captain, we have finished installing the new container field cover. It looks like it's going to work for us. However..."

He stalled, and Xander continued, "You don't think we'll get more than one jump out of her?"

He tilted his head in astonishment. "That's correct, sir."

Xander moved under the main reactor and found the new containment field cover. He ran his wrinkled fingers over it momentarily and then went to the nearest control screen. He punched up some technical data and skimmed through it.

"Can I find something for you, Captain?"

Xander continued pushing around icons and menus as he spoke.

"Commander Qin and I go way back. Did you know that?"

Culler shook his head, his angelic face the embodiment of innocence.

"You don't remain close personal friends with an Engineer and not pick up on some things. I've heard him lecture his stokers and then drone on about them to me for hours. Anyway, the upshot was that some of what he told me stuck in the dark recesses of my old brain."

He called up a section of the procedure manual for *Weippe's* engine to find what he was looking for.

"Here, read through this. Qin wrote the book on how this mess all works; he just never told anyone. Everything you'll need to know about this star drive and how it interfaces with the tunnel drive is at your fingertips. When you read it, you can even hear his craggy old voice in your head."

Cullers examined the manual and started smiling.

"Thank you, sir!"

Xander patted him on the back and headed back to the galley.

***

Xander polished off his breakfast in record time, prompting Odem to ask if he wanted seconds. The cook waited for the Captain to shake his head before topping off his coffee. Lieutenant Vance swung through, stopping to acknowledge the Captain.

"Good morning, sir."

"Morning, Number One. Lieutenant Boxer mentioned that she had found odd readings in the long-range scans. She wanted you to look into them today."

Vance bit his lip as he nodded. "I'll take a look at them, sir."

"Good. Let's meet for lunch in the wardroom along with the project seconds," Xander added before Vance left the room.

"Aye, sir. See you then."

Xander shook his head as he stood up to leave. Odem cleared his plate as more crewmen arrived for their first meal.

****

The bridge was quiet when the Captain finally made it on deck. There were just a couple of petty officers at key stations. Xander took his seat and started going over the shift log. Again, the image of a dying Qin returned to his mind's eye. *Why won't my head let him go?*

Nothing seemed amiss in the log, prompting him to look at the primary screen. It showed the gas giant staring back at them as if they owed it thanks for not having killed them. Boxer echoed, "There are some odd readings on the long-range scans." He punched up the long-range scans and started poking around at the returns he couldn't identify. Most of it was just interstellar background noise. Distant novas, pops and clicks of storms at the gas giant, things every Scanning Officer is taught to ignore.

He checked the contact log and immediately found what Boxer had annotated. Roughly every nine minutes, a repeating signal seemed closer than it should be. It seemed to cycle randomly through a dozen different frequencies, occurring naturally.

He messed with the isolation controls but could not pinpoint the signal or guess where it would occur again.

Eventually, he grew bored with it and switched to a live scan. After listening intently to the scanner for nearly ten minutes, he passed it off to Boxer's shift replacement and went on to other concerns.

***

Five hours into the shift, Lieutenant Vance came onto the bridge, still wearing his spacesuit. He stood over his station and relieved the duty NCO. Plopping down into the seat, he yawned before slipping on the headphones.

The captain was busy calculating possible return tunnel jumps and didn't even notice Vance's entrance. The strange rotating signal echoed inside Vance's head as he listened. It was like nothing he had ever heard before. The signal strength oscillated almost as much as the tone. It reminded him of when he was a kid and played with his uncle's shortwave radios. They would hear signals coming from the other side of the world, and sometimes, when the conditions were right, they'd hear signals from the moon or one of the other nearby planets.

Vance fine-tuned around the signal, and for a brief moment, it came in clear as a klaxon. He stood up reflexively. The other crewmen looked at him, sensing alarm. The captain was too deep in his calculations to have noticed.

"Captain, I think I know what that signal is."

Xander pulled himself away and looked over at his second in command.

"It's a beacon, sir!"

Xander raised an eyebrow. "You mean it's not a natural phenomenon?"

Vance's face was pallid, even in the dim light.

"I think the Blue-Devils are calling for reinforcements."

Xander stood up and came over to Vance's station. Vance pointed to his screens. "See how it repeats the same three tones and then waits for about nine minutes until repeating a different set of tones? That's exactly how our navigation beacons work."

Xander muttered something under his breath that sounded to Vance like a curse. He reached over and activated Vance's PA controls.

"Attention the ship, this is the Captain. We're going back to Condition Red, repeat, Condition Red."

When he announced the threat condition, the ship's computers activated the alarms and turned the bridge lights back to red.

"We have to find that transmitter and take it out before it attracts more of those giant starships to this system," Xander said, the urgency in his voice clear to everyone.

Vance sat back down and started triangulating the signal. He needed Helm's help to get the ship moving in another direction. "Helm, come to four, six, fiver, and increase speed."

"Helm, aye, sir."

The ambient sound increased as the primary drive spun up, and the ship swung to a new course.

"New course completed," the Helmsman said.

"Keep us here for twenty minutes."

"Aye, sir."

Vance continued to search for the beacon. At the nine-minute mark, he reacquired the signal again. The transmission was clear and strong, so the source had to be nearby. He had the location after giving the computer a few moments to triangulate.

"The transmitter is a few hundred meters off our port," Vance stated.

"Helm, take us there," Captain Xander ordered, returning to his seat.

"Aye, Captain. Estimated arrival in fifteen minutes," the acting Helmsman said.

The *Weippe* steered toward the signal, and Vance focused the close-field sensors to acquire it. When he had an image, he transferred it to the main viewer.

The object was about the size of a refrigerator and spun on its axis. It looked to Vance like a spinning child's top.

"Weapons, do we have anything we can shoot at that thing?" Xander asked.

The kid manning the controls in Boxer's absence smiled. "Aye, sir. We have six rounds created from scrap metal, but they are untested."

Xander glanced back at Vance, who shrugged.

"Let's test them. Punch some holes in that thing."

"Aye, Captain."

The newly minted steel nails were loaded into the main gun, which swung around to point into the void in the transmitter's direction.

"Target acquired, rounds loaded."

Xander pointed to the growing image on the main viewer. "Fire!"

The deck rumbled as the railgun fired its rounds into the void. The target continued to spin and sputter random messages until the rounds hit and completely blew it apart. There was an initial blast from its power source, followed by nothing but a fine spray of metal particles.

"Nice shooting," Xander offered. The kid smiled from ear to ear as he looked around the bridge. "Thank you, sir."

"How fast can you produce more rounds?" The kid looked down and double-checked his controls before answering.

"Looks like we have enough resources to build six per shift. I used only two for that shot."

Xander and Vance nodded to each other. "Excellent, keep making them. Let Lieutenant Vance know if you need more scrap and or personnel."

"Aye, sir."

Vance returned to his wide-field scans. The system was young, and there were an unusual number of proto-planetary objects, comets, and chunks of rock. It would not be easy to see any ship approaching it.

"Helm, take us back to the ring and slide us into a gap in the ice," Captain Xander said, returning to his tunnel jump calculations.

The *Weippe* slowly headed towards the gas giant again, like a traumatized person returning to the scene of a terrible accident.

Chapter 21

Captain Xander was the first to arrive in the wardroom for lunch. Odem was at his station, ready with water and a fresh cup of coffee. Xander was distracted by the data on his tablet. Things were not shaping up well for their return jumps. It was the topic of his meeting, and he wasn't sure how to inform them. His eyes clouded as he stared through the numbers on the flat screen. The face of Qin returned to his mind's eye. *What are you trying to tell me, old friend?* Qin's face remained still as a death mask.

Lieutenant Vance entered the room and sat beside the captain, snapping him out of his haze.

"What's for lunch, sir?"

"Huh? Oh, cold cuts again. I'm sure."

Vance made a face as Odem brought him a cold drink.

"I can arrange for some leftover sausages if you like," Odem said.

"No, thanks."

The other petty officer, Cullers, arrived with the stand-in helmsman. They had never been in the room before.

"Welcome to how the other side lives, gentlemen," Vance greeted them.

They both took their seats, looking nervous about dining in officer country. Odem served them cold cuts and cheese with ice water. No bread was provided, but a platter with various crackers sufficed.

Vance motioned for the NCOs to dig in as he helped himself. Captain Xander took a sip of his coffee and launched right into it. He was the type to prefer straight talk to beating around the bush. Rip the bandage off rather than pick around the edges, forever extending the removal process.

"We have enough fuel for only one tunnel jump."

Everyone stopped what they were doing and looked at Xander.

"I've crunched the numbers repeatedly, and that's the best I can do. We can't go home. At least not directly."

Vance finished chewing and raised a finger. "Where are we going to jump to then?"

Xander's face was as pallid as his white beard. "Ostrov system or Jhana out past Syndal."

Ostrov was closer to their current position, but little was known about it. Theoretically, there could be a habitable planet in the red star system, but nothing was on the charts. Jhana was a long way from their current position and closer to the Federation. At least it had one habitable planet orbiting a blue-gas giant. Neither system had an established Federation presence nor indigenous sentient life.

Vance continued eating as he considered his options. Xander grabbed a few pieces of ham and set them on top of a cracker. He added a condiment and shoved it into his mouth.

"There are no Federation settlements in either system, sir," Cullers stated.

"Aye, that's the rub, son," Xander said with his mouth full.

Vance took a swig of water and cleared his throat. "Jhana is a long shot. We'd be in tunnel space for nearly a week. I'm not sure we have the rations to make it. Not to mention what we could find in the system to live on."

Xander nodded in agreement.

"Ostrov isn't far, but we know of no known habitable worlds there."

Xander was going to speak, but Cullers beat him out. "Ostrov has two suns. Maybe the sister star has a wider life belt."

Xander pointed to Cullers. "Good observation. I thought of that, though. Our most recent scans of Ostrov One have revealed only five planets, all outside the life belt save for one. But it's small and doesn't have much of an atmosphere. Probably no liquid water."

The conversation leveled off as everyone ate their meal. After a while, Petty Officer Cullers cleared his throat and spoke up. "Captain, if I may?"

Xander motioned for him to continue.

"My family owns a spice hauler, and we used to make runs to the Outer Rim. We've been as far out as Plaue, only a few light years from Jhana. There's a planet in the Plaue system with an outpost called Flaellen that we could contact for help."

Xander and Vance locked eyes briefly, and then the Captain said, "Cullers, how big is that outpost? I mean, do they have anything that could get to Plaue?"

Cullers shook his head. "Unknown, sir. It's been maybe five years since I was there. At the time, it was pretty rugged but self-sufficient."

"Odem, could you join us for a moment?" Vance asked.

Odem exited his preparation area, wiping his hands on a towel.

"How much food do we have in stores? I need to know how many days we can stay alive, assuming no resupply."

Odem nodded and then looked up at the low ceiling in thought.

"Sir, we had enough food to feed fifty people for a month. We've only been out here a week or so. Plus, we've lost some people, so that should give us a few weeks' rations before my cupboards run dry."

Vance nodded and looked back to the Captain. Xander was slowly stroking his beard in thought.

"That gives us a week to get there and a week or so to hold out until we can be rescued," Vance reasoned.

Xander nodded. "I think we can do that. What bothers me is how transitory outposts can be. We won't know if they have a ship that can reach us until we contact them."

Everyone began putting down their food, as if not eating it now would somehow let them eat for another day down the line.

"This is classified information, but the Surface Army anxiously awaits our return. We were supposed to make four tunnel jumps before arriving back at Allifax. Our secondary return point was to be Dania. There's probably a contingent of troops there. But I can't figure out how to get us near there without leaving a trail back to the Federation."

Xander paused for a moment.

"What was the third return point, sir? There's always more than one backup plan," Vance said.

Xander scanned the faces of his crew before answering.

"Santos. It's another two light-years from Plaue."

Vance slapped the table with his hand. "That's good, right? They'll hear our SOS from the other side of Plaue and send a ship for us."

Xander shook his head.

"Fort Santone has no space dock. It's a tiny scientific outpost."

"Shit."

"We're back to hoping Plaue has a ship," Xander said.

Xander wiped his mouth with his napkin and stood up. Everyone else stood at attention.

"We'll proceed to Jhana when the tunnel drive is repaired. Until then, light rations for everyone."

***

Vance found himself in space again late in his shift. He was finishing up rerouting some electrical cables through the repaired beam. Alone in the quiet of his suit, he could hear his breathing and an occasional air circulation fan blowing in his helmet. He finished making a welded joint and pushed back against his safety line. Turning to his right, he looked at the scrambled chunks of ice and rock that made up the ring. It was twice as thick as the *Weippe* and served as a good wall to hide behind, provided nobody was looking at you from above or below the ring.

Some of the ice chunks were as small as handballs. He had to fight the urge to skirt over to them and see how far he could throw one. With little gravity, he reasoned he could chuck it pretty far. The distant red star of the system filtered light through the rusty, organic-rich ice of the ring.

Off in the distance was a small shepherd moon of the rings. It was easily twice the size of the *Weippe*. Beyond that was the gas giant itself. Nobody had formally named it, but those outside the ship started calling it Aeolus, after an ancient god of wind.

"Sir, this is Jenkins at Scanning." The loud voice, coming from his helmet, startled Vance.

"Go, Jenkins."

"I'm getting strange signals on the close-range set. They look similar to the readings we got for that Blue-Devil ship."

Vance rolled over and started wrapping up his business before heading back inside. As he fumbled for his tethered instruments, the bright light of the nearby red star was occluded. He glanced out at the ring and saw a triangular shadow cast across the ice chunks.

"Jenkins, that's them; they're back. How many targets do you have?"

There was a pause as Jenkins probably notified the captain. Vance continued collecting his tools and headed back towards the only working airlock.

"I have two contacts approaching from separate grid points."

"Two? I'm coming in," Vance said as he slid down the narrow side of the *Weippe* and approached the airlock hatch.

When Vance cycled through the airlock, Sergeant Rizzo was waiting for him. His dark face was bleary-eyed from sleep. The ship was at action stations, and alarms were screaming all down the ship's narrow corridors.

"I think we're ready. Get to Engineering and see if you can help them. I have to get to the bridge," Vance hollered over the noise.

Rizzo helped him out of his suit and then headed off toward Engineering. Vance ran down the starboard corridor, hooking up with Lieutenant Lestor as she exited her cabin. Her hair was a mess, but she was at least wearing a clean uniform.

"Can't you guys keep the racket down while I sleep?"

"Sorry," was all Vance had time to say as he sprinted up the ladder to the bridge level.

They both entered the bridge together, replacing the crewmen at their stations.

"Number One, I'm heading for open space at full speed," Captain Xander calmly stated.

"Aye, sir. Two contacts, one at four hundred kilometers, the other at eight hundred. Looks like the same kind of ship we defeated."

Xander watched the grainy video images on a split screen on the primary monitor. "Damn, they're huge," he said as he clicked the intercom.

"Engineering, how soon can we tunnel jump?"

Petty Officer Cullers responded, "Spinning up the T-drive now. We should be ready in ten minutes."

"Shit, we'll all be dead by then. Give me full speed on the main."

"Aye, sir."

Lieutenant Lestor found coordinates streaming into her system. She glanced up to see Xander staring at her. "Sent you our jump coordinates."

She reread them, this time aloud. "Jhana system, sir?"

"Is there a problem, Lieutenant?"

She furrowed her dark eyebrows and shook her head.

"No, sir. Setting the course."

Xander continued looking at her. She hadn't been to the meeting where they decided where to jump. There was a chance she knew something they all didn't.

"You don't seem convinced that's a good choice," Xander offered.

"Sorry, Captain. I didn't think there was anything there."

"There's not. But we can send an SOS to Plaue and hope they have a tunnel ship that can reach us."

Lestor nodded. "Okay, thanks."

Xander gave her one final look, and since she had nothing further to add, he turned back to the main viewer.

"Alien ships closing. At their current speed, they will be in firing range in six minutes," Vance offered.

Xander pounded his armrest. The intercom switched on from the impact. "Engineering, we need to jump ASAP!"

Both alien ships were getting larger on the viewer. The closest one's forward weapon ports began to glow.

"The lead ship is getting ready to fire," Vance said.

"Weapons, arm up the guns and lock onto the lead ship. We will attempt a lateral spin to confuse their targeting system."

"Helm, aye."

"Weapons locked, Captain. We have twelve shots."

Xander shook his head, but he'd take it over nothing at all.

"Engineering, how much longer?"

"Five minutes, sir."

Xander pointed back to Lestor and motioned in a circle with his hand. She took manual control of the Corvette and started spinning and turning at random angles to make it a difficult target.

The *Weippe* groaned a bit on the inside as she rotated around. Her main guns constantly adjusted for a new target as she ran hard in the opposite direction of the approaching burned-orange starships.

"Incoming rounds, brace for impact," Vance hollered.

The first round impacted somewhere astern as the whole Corvette shook and rattled from the energy. As the ship rang like a bell, Xander opened the intercom to Engineering.

"We still good for the jump?"

"Aye, Captain. We need to level out to make the navigation bearings," Lestor said, the tone in her voice echoing Commander Qin.

Xander pointed to Lester again. "Level out and make your jump."

She nodded as she coaxed her controls. The *Weippe* made one last tight turn, putting them on a course to intercept the incoming alien ships.

"We're heading right towards them!" Xander exclaimed.

"Time to jump, ten seconds," Lestor replied.

Vance interjected, "New rounds are incoming. Time to impact eight seconds."

It was going to be damn close, and everyone on the bridge knew it. On the primary monitor, the alien ships were so near you could make out rectangular portholes lit red from inside. Vance wondered if they thought the *Weippe* had suddenly turned suicidal in charging them.

"Weapons, let 'em have it!"

"Firing, sir."

Some of the *Weippe's* rounds hit the incoming ball of glowing energy from the alien ship but did little to dissuade it from coming at the *Weippe*. The tiny Corvette shuddered again as the tunnel drive activated.

Everything shifted as the *Weippe* fell into an artificial wormhole and winked out of existence.

Chapter 22

The bridge of the *Weippe* was tranquil in tunnel space. Air circulation fans whirred, and the main drive hummed, but it all seemed quieter than before the jump. Vance knew it was probably just in his head, but being in tunnel space was still unnerving. It was so far out of the normal realm of experience that his mind sometimes refused to believe it was happening.

Outside, there was nothing. Just inky blackness that had no light from distant stars. It was like being in a light-tight bag without knowing which direction you were heading or even moving. Navigation inside a tunnel was impossible. You set your course, predicted the time you would have to be inside to get where you were going, and then exited at that time. If you dropped out of the tunnel early or late, you could be hundreds of light-years from where you wanted to be.

The main viewer showed the countdown until they dropped out of the tunnel in large segmented numbers. They would be inside this bubble for seven days and six nights, closed off from the rest of the universe, unable to communicate with anyone or see anything out in the crushing darkness.

"We are on course, and the timer's running, sir," said Lestor.

Captain Xander let out an audible sigh of relief.

Vance's scanners were inoperative until they emerged from the tunnel. He started shutting them down to conserve power, then noticed a contact in front of them. His heart sank as he recognized its shape and size.

"Captain!" he exclaimed without thinking.

"Yes?"

"I think we pulled in the nearest Blue-Devil ship!"

Vance put his scans on the primary monitor. The shape was precise as a heat signature. He switched on the optical and turned on the floodlights on the bow. Everyone on the bridge gasped at once. There was the ship that had been attacking them, floating at an odd angle in the darkness.

"Scan them, see if they are alive in there," Xander ordered as he stood up and approached Vance's station.

"I'm picking up something alive over there."

Xander stroked his beard and looked back at the ghostly image on the main viewer.

"I've seen this happen once before. We dragged a tug into a tunnel when I was on the *Gratier*. Killed everyone aboard when it fell out."

Vance was amazed. He'd never heard of this happening before.

"Watch for weapon activation. Once they figure out what happened, I guess they will attack us to get out," Xander said.

"What if they don't, sir? They could ride it out and attack after we return to normal space."

Xander looked down at him, his brow rising slowly. "We can't drag them back to Plaue. They'd destroy us and then be a stone's throw from the Federation."

Xander looked back at the screen. "How the hell did they manage to get in here with us? They must have closed on us in the final seconds."

Vance could hear the respect and even admiration in his voice.

"Do you think they realized what we were doing and purposely dove into the tunnel?"

Xander shook his head. "No, I don't think they could have understood what we were doing in time."

He looked back down at Vance with concern in his gray eyes.

"We have to drop them out. Now, before they figure out what's happened," Vance said.

"If we drop out of the tunnel, we'll be stranded," Lestor pleaded from behind them.

Xander seemed stumped for what to do, avoiding eye contact with anyone. Vance turned around to face Lestor. "Helm, get us closer. I want our nose against their hull."

Lestor's face knotted in confusion. "Sir?"

Vance moved back to his seat and stared up at the viewer.

"Just do it. We're going to push them out of the tunnel."

Lestor looked to Xander for validation. The old man nodded for her to do it. She shook her head and took over the controls.

"Tunnels are only so big. Their tails have got to be damn close to the stream. If we can nudge them over, they might fall out, and we won't," Vance explained.

Lestor was unconvinced, but she edged closer to the massive orange starship. Predictably, the ship responded by backing away and facing them, its weapon ports glowing.

"Keep going. They might just run themselves out," Xander said.

The *Weippe* closed quickly, and the massive ship started to shudder. Pieces of its drives broke apart, and the entire vessel winked out of existence in a flash of red light. They were alone again in the darkness.

Xander snapped his fingers and turned to face Vance.

"How's our hull integrity?"

Vance scanned his screens and looked up. "Nominal. The repair job is holding."

"Engineering, this is the Captain. Everything okay back there?"

Cullers responded quickly. "Aye, sir. Tunnel drive steady and holding."

"Acknowledged."

Xander let out another sigh and shook his head. Then he pointed to Vance with a grin. "Nice work, Lieutenant."

Vance nodded back at him. All those years of studying tunnel physics in school paid off. The tunnel created a bubble in space that was only so big. As long as you didn't rupture or slip out of the bubble, you were propelled through space and time over great distances. But if you popped the bubble or fell out of it, your ship departed controlled space. In other words, you were destroyed.

***

Life eventually settled into a routine for the remainder of the voyage home. The *Weippe* cruised with few technical issues, and the crew went about the regular business of being in space. There were grim reminders of how costly the mission had been everywhere you went on board. There was also the absence of friends and coworkers who had not returned.

Vance spent more time with his two remaining lieutenants than he might otherwise have done. Having survived together made them closer to one another as spacers and as people. Mealtime conversations with the captain in the wardroom were more personal than on other starships he had been on. Captain Xander took more interest in their family lives and future endeavors. Sometimes during the evening meals, he broke into the limited supply of wine and insisted on regaling the younger officers with tales from his long and interesting career in the Fleet.

At the start of the mission, Vance had been less interested in hearing what the senior officers had to say. It had seemed to him that they were living in the past, and their better days were long behind them. He hadn't seen much value in their stories, some of which were only amusing to Qin and Xander. Now, he looked forward to the downtime and the Captain's off-color and often silly adventures in the ancient days of the Federation Fleet.

One evening, after the other officers had retired, Vance and Xander sat together in the wardroom talking. As Xander's story ended, Vance had almost finished his wine and slowly rolled the glass in his hand.

Xander studied him briefly and then asked, "Vance, why are you humoring me by listening to my old stories? The others had enough sense to turn in, but here you are."

Vance sat down the glass and shrugged. The wine had relaxed him, and he wasn't hungry—just content.

"I guess I've grown fond of your stories, sir. I'll admit, when I first came aboard, I didn't want to be here much."

Xander winked at him. "Stuck on an old ship with an even older captain."

Vance nodded. "Something like that, yes." He sat up and thought for a moment.

"I've seen what this old ship and her captain can do now. I'm both impressed and humbled."

Xander smiled to himself and shakily stood up. He motioned to the surrounding ship.

"She's a damn fine boat, that's for sure. And she'll keep you alive and get you home if you treat her well. Never forget that."

Vance stood up. "I won't, sir."

"Good night, Number One," Xander said as he left the room.

"Good night, Captain."

After being alone in the room, Vance picked up his wineglass and held it in the air.

"To the *SS Weippe*," he said as he drank the last swallow of wine.

***

On the seventh day in tunnel space, the *Weippe* dropped out of her dark womb and into standard space. A brilliant blue-white star shone on the main viewer. Vance glanced to his right and saw stars out the porthole after what seemed like a lifetime. For the first time in his career, it was a welcome sight. The longest he'd ever been in tunnel space was a day or two, and coming out after a whole week was akin to being born into the light again or awakening from a long, terrible dream.

"Helm, do you have your bearings?" Captain Xander asked.

Lieutenant Lestor looked up with a grin on her face.

"Aye, sir. We are in the Jhana system."

"Outstanding. Lieutenant Vance, get on the horn and see if we can raise anyone."

Vance was already tuning his transmitter and slewing the antenna into place. "Aye, Captain."

Xander switched on the intercom. "Bridge to Engineering. How are we looking, Cullers?"

Petty Officer Cullers responded with his usual professionalism.

"Tunnel drive is winding down. The main is lit and good to go, Captain."

"Outstanding. Bridge out."

Xander stood up and walked over to the single porthole on the port side. He stared out at the infiniteness of stars. Xander briefly thought about his fondness for the stars, like an ancient mariner fondly recalling the glassy waves of a tropical sea. He stood there deep in thought for a while, staring out the thick glass.

"Sir, I've made contact with Flaellen."

Xander turned away from the porthole to look at Vance.

"Well, do they have a tunnel-drive ship?"

"Yes!"

Chapter 23

During the trip back to their home port of Allifax, Xander and Vance never discussed their mission. They didn't discuss the *Wayfinder*, the Blue-Devils, or what happened during combat or evasive maneuvers. It wasn't that Vance didn't want to. He wanted many questions answered, but he could tell the old man was unwilling to entertain them. At least not until they were safely back in port.

The *Weippe* cruised into the docks at Allifax a week and a half after arriving in Federation space. Most of her crew had been transferred off the ship, and only a handful remained to steer her back to port.

Vance was on the bridge as the ship was put to bed, and moorings secured. Lieutenant Lestor was the only other person on deck with him when they came to a complete stop. "Engineering, bridge. Shut her down, Cullers."

"Aye, sir. It's good to be home."

Vance and Lestor exchanged knowing looks. "Yes, it is. Bridge out."

"Do you have any family here to see you back?" Vance asked.

"No, sir. I've already contacted my mom and dad about my return."

Vance nodded. He would ask if she wanted to join him and the other officers at the dockside restaurant. It would be their first real food in a long time, but the intercom buzz interrupted him.

"Vance, please meet me in my cabin when you finish."

Lestor raised an eyebrow, and Vance shrugged. Maybe he finally wanted to do his after-action report.

"Aye, sir."

Lestor changed from her station to another, shutting down the bridge consoles. She had drawn the short straw in overseeing the repairs. Everyone else left on board would be heading down for planet leave.

"Lieutenant, would you mind joining me and the other officers for dinner tonight? Before we all scatter and go our separate ways?"

"You mean real food, sir? Of course. You buying?"

"The drinks, yes."

"I'll be there," she said, her face relaxing into a warm smile that he hadn't seen since the last time they were in port.

***

Vance knocked on the metal hatch to the Captain's cabin once, and Xander opened it to let him in. He motioned for Vance to have a seat on the stripped bunk mattress.

"I don't normally do our after-action reports until we are back in port and the crew has mostly gone. Keeps the chance of our being overheard low since just about everything we say is classified," Xander began.

Vance gave him his undivided attention. Xander sat at his desk and slowly stroked his beard a few times before starting.

"My orders for this mission were in two parts. You already know the first part: find and, if need be, help the crew of the *Wayfinder*. But I had a second mission that only Major Bray and I were privy to. We were to seek out and engage the Blue-Devils to learn their weaknesses and strengths. That's why we installed the big rail gun, and that's why Bray's team was armed to the teeth."

When he paused, Vance interrupted.

"Sir, why weren't I and the other officers informed of this mission?"

Xander sighed.

"Fleet bullshit about compartmentalizing information. We're all military, and we're expected to fight when told. Someone above my pay grade figured you didn't need to know any more than you did."

Vance frowned. He didn't care for that explanation but respected the Captain enough not to complain.

"We knew they were going to be out there. We just didn't know how fearsome they would be."

Vance held up his hand, and Xander held short.

"I don't understand why they sent a Corvette instead of a front-line battleship. We were in way over our heads out there, sir."

"I know. Look, maybe Fleet didn't want to show their hand? Tip them off about what kind of firepower we have?"

Vance reluctantly agreed that that was probably a smart call.

"I've been in here the whole way back, filing intelligence reports on their capabilities. When I leave this ship, the Surface Army will probably debrief me for days until they get all the necessary intel."

Vance nudged his head. "Then what, sir? Will they start beefing up the fleet's ships, knowing what we do about them?"

Xander shook his head. "Probably not. I suspect this will all blow over in a few weeks and we'll be back on regular patrols like nothing happened. If we're lucky, we might get to keep the gun," he pointed behind them.

Now, it was Vance's turn to shake his head in frustration.

Xander glanced out his single porthole. You could just see the top of the *SS Darguare*, one of the latest Destroyers from the inner systems.

"Did you catch a glimpse of that beauty?" he asked, pointing to the porthole.

Vance glanced over his shoulder at it and shook it off.

"She doesn't have anything on the *Weippe*, sir."

Xander started to chuckle. Vance didn't see any humor in what he had said.

"When you first came aboard, you thought this boat was an old scrap heap. You thought maybe someone in Fleet had it in for you."

Vance relaxed a bit as Xander continued to chuckle.

"After what we've been through, sir. Can you blame me?"

Xander opened a drawer and pulled out a pair of silver clusters. He stood up and slid his ankles together at attention. Vance jumped up quickly, expecting his captain to dismiss him.

"Lieutenant Armon Vance, it is my duty to inform you that you have been promoted to Lieutenant Commander by order of the Federation Fleet, Admiral Irvin C. Kain, commanding officer."

Vance couldn't hide the shock as Xander shook his hand and handed him his new rank. He looked down at the shiny metal clusters in his hand and remembered to salute the captain.

Xander saluted him back and then turned to gather up his duffel bag.

"What are you waiting for, Commander? You'd better pin those on and get back on your bridge."

"My… my bridge, sir?"

"She's all yours now, kid. Don't break her keel."

Vance was still dumbfounded. Now, the empty cabin was starting to make sense. It was his cabin now. It was his boat.

He quickly pinned on his new rank and then saluted Captain Xander again.

Xander shook his hand firmly.

"Where are you heading, sir? If I may ask."

Xander frowned as he sighed. "I'm flying west to reside over a desk until they put me out to pasture. I have only a few months until I retire."

Vance held the handshake for another heartfelt pull.

"It was an honor and a pleasure serving with you, Captain."

"The same, Commander. Don't forget what you learned on this voyage; it will save your ass sometime."

Vance smiled as they let go, and Xander left the tiny room.

***

The starport restaurant was called Last Chance. For many spacers heading out into the void, it would be their last chance to have a decent meal or a stiff drink. Lieutenants Boxer and Lester sat at a booth overlooking a large glass window with a nice view of Starship Row, where all the fleet ships were docked. The *Weippe* was down in front, looking as severe as any active duty ship.

Boxer was dressed in her gray duty uniform, making her the odd one out at the table. Vance and Lestor both wore Fleet black dress uniforms. They had each ordered something different from the varied menu and were leisurely finishing up their last bites.

"So, when did the old man promote you?" Boxer asked after nobody had mentioned it during dinner.

"Today. Although I checked, and the document was signed before we left."

Lester put down her fork and picked up her glass of wine. "Why did he wait until you returned to give you your pins?"

Vance shook his head slowly. "He probably didn't want it to affect our mission."

Boxer chimed in, "I can see that. Your head wouldn't have been able to fit through the *Weippe's* hatches."

"Thanks," Vance said, taking a drink of his beer.

"So, do you have new orders yet?" Lestor asked.

Before Vance could answer, Captain Xander approached their table. They all started to get up, but he waved for them to remain seated.

"May I join you, folks?"

Vance slid over to make room for him at the booth. A worn service android appeared and asked if Xander wanted to order something.

"I'll have a scotch and water, please."

The off-white android nodded and left.

"I wanted to stop by and thank you for your service. I'm shipping out to Selene soon."

"You're not staying for the repairs, Captain?" Lestor asked.

Xander smiled and looked over at Vance. "That's his problem now. I'm heading out to pasture."

Vance smirked as Lestor and Boxer both realized who their new captain was.

Boxer was sitting beside Vance, and she extended a firm handshake. "Congratulations, sir."

"Thanks."

Lestor tipped her head to him and smiled. "I don't suppose you need a new FO, Commander?"

Vance locked eyes with her. "I was hoping you would stay on."

She looked down at her plate and then out the window at the worn-down and broken Corvette. "I don't know; that rusty old boat isn't my idea of a proper starship."

He smiled, appreciating her echoing his thoughts when he first came aboard the *Weippe*.

Boxer was a bit slow on the uptake. She looked at Lestor as if he were crazy. Lester smiled back at her and Vance.

"Point taken, Number One," Vance said.

Xander chuckled as he looked out at the *Weippe*. He would miss that old boat, and everyone at the table knew it. The android returned with his drink, and Vance interjected. "Put it on my tab."

Xander tipped his glass to the newly minted commander. Vance held up his drink for a toast.

"To Captain Xander, the Fleet's finest!"

Everyone clinked glasses and took a drink.

Xander held up his glass again. "To Commander Qin, Major Bray, Lieutenant Torven, and all those who didn't make it back."

They all echoed, "Aye, sir," and clinked their glasses before taking another drink.

Boxer turned to Vance and nudged him.

"To the new Captain of the *Weippe*, Commander Vance,"

Lestor added, "May he never falter in the face of pirates and bring his herd home."

They all took another drink. Captain Xander looked at his watch and set his drink glass down as he slid out of the booth.

"I should probably be leaving. Take care, you guys, and drop me a line sometime. I'll have all the time in the world to read dispatches."

Everyone stood up as he walked away. When he was gone, they all sat back down and relaxed.

"What do you think Fleet will do about what we saw?" Boxer asked.

"You mean the Blue-Devils?"

She nodded, and Vance looked back out the window. "I suspect Fleet will do its best to bury it in operational security, and we'll never hear about it again. That's pretty much how the bureaucracy works."

Lestor sighed. "We won't be able to talk about it. Like it never happened."

Boxer swore, "Oh, it happened, and we won't forget it."

They all nodded in unison and fell silent.

Boxer looked over at Vance and studied him until he noticed her stare and looked back at her. "One thing has changed. They're assigning SA soldiers on all fleet ships, effective immediately."

"That's good. Because we're getting another railgun and armor as part of our repairs."

Boxer grinned from ear to ear. She loved big guns.

Chapter 24

Captain Xander sat back in his padded chair and kicked his feet up on his expansive wooden desk. His office was twice as big as his cabin aboard the *Weippe,* and it felt like he was sitting in a stadium. Outside his window, the Ostrov mountain range, snow-capped and majestic in the distance, was visible. The spartan office had no decorations, just a terminal screen, keyboard, and a Corvette model he had purchased at a nearby hobby shop.

He intended to spend the next few months building the kit instead of doing anything other than the bare necessities of his job. When he was done, he would have a visual reminder of his last command: The tiny little boat with the best crew in the fleet and the most formidable hull ever built.

He reached down to his old, worn duffel bag, pulled a sword, and rested it on his lap. It was the Blue-Devil falchion presented to him by Major Bray. He had smuggled it off the ship and neglected to inform Fleet that he had kept it. It was the only tangible proof of what he and his crew had endured on his final mission.

The blade was wide and still razor sharp. It had a blue tint to the metal and would make a pleasing presentation piece in his office. He ran a hand over the flat side of the blade, remembering the actions that had led to too many deaths on that voyage. Fleet had partly used the casualties as evidence that he was too old to captain a starship. The after-action reports, meanwhile, completely covered up the fact that the *Weippe* and its crew had successfully destroyed two Blue-Devil starships, each three times their size. *To hell with them, he thought. I know what we did; my crew knows what we did, and they will never forget it. They will run into those blue-skinned bastards again someday, and when they do, all hell will break loose.*

The image of Commander Qin's irradiated body came back to him as he looked at his reflection in the blade. Poor Qin. He deserved a better, more honorable death. Xander remembered a conversation he had had with Qin on an earlier mission. Somehow, they had gotten onto how they wished to die. Xander insisted on leading his crew into combat, going down with the ship like some ancient mariner. But Qin was more thoughtful and reflective. As he was at such times of honest contemplation, Qin said that he didn't care how he died as long as it was in service to others.

Xander's frown was reflected back at him in the blade. Qin had undoubtedly fulfilled his desire in that regard. He had saved Engineering and all those aboard the *Weippe* by his heroic actions.

Xander reached back into his bag, pulled out two polished black wooden blocks, and set them on the expansive desk. Then he placed the blade on them and sat back to look at it. The alien hands that crafted such a beautiful weapon would be a worthy opponent in future conflicts. A conflict he hoped he'd never live to see.

***

Lieutenant Boxer stood on the lowest deck of the *Weippe* and looked down at the pit that held the newly installed railgun. She was dressed in her gray duty uniform as she leaned on the railing. The freshly painted gray metal of the weapon contrasted with the worn, old gray paint of the hull. The gun was completely automated and had an even greater firing rate than the one installed on the top deck of the Corvette.

Such a fine railgun would completely overpower any pirate ship she had ever seen. This weapon was not designed to keep the peace. It was a weapon of war. But she was damn glad to have it, knowing what she did about what lurked beyond the fringes of the Federation.

A man approached her and snapped off a salute. She turned to see Sergeant Rizzo's warm smile. She returned the salute.

"Reporting for duty, ma'am," Rizzo said.

Boxer shook his hand. "It's good to have you with us again, Rizzo."

"I wouldn't ship out with any other crew, ma'am."

Having survived the ordeal of combat, they looked at each other as only comrades in arms could. Finally, Boxer motioned to the new gun.

"She's got twice the velocity of the old one and a higher rate of fire. The Fleet is trying to ensure we're ready for more than pirates."

Rizzo looked down at the automated loading mechanism. "Do you think she'll take rounds fashioned from deck metal?"

Both of them chuckled momentarily before Boxer started to wonder whether it would or not. She had recommended that in her after-action report but figured it would be too soon to see those changes. It would take the gun manufacturers a while to design that feature into new models.

She looked back at the Rizzo. "You bring any fun new toys with you this time?"

He grinned back at her. "A few. Would you like to see them, ma'am"?

"You know it."

***

Commander Vance sat at the galley table and sipped a black coffee. Cook Odem was grilling him a ham and egg omelet, which filled the narrow room with a delicious aroma.

A young Engineer entered the room looking a bit confused. He sat down across from Vance at the table. "Why are we here instead of at our posts, Commander? The ship is launching now."

Vance smiled and set his mug down.

"Tradition, Lieutenant Jones. Tradition."

***

Lieutenant Lestor sat in the *Weippe's* captain's chair and surveyed the bridge. There were new faces and a few old familiar ones at each station. The small command center of the Corvette had undergone computer and sensor upgrades, but it was still the same worn-down paint and exposed conduits that it had always been. She could hear the air circulation fans whirling and feel the main drive thrumming under her feet. It was good to be going out again. *It's good to be home.*

"All moorings cleared, ma'am," said the Helmsman.

"Acknowledged."

She clicked the intercom button. "Bridge to Engineering. Everything all set back there, Mr. Cullers?"

"Aye, ma'am. Main is spun up and thrusters primed."

"Outstanding. Helm, back us out. Please."

The Helmsman hesitated, and Lestor looked back at him.

"Problem, Lieutenant?"

"Shouldn't the Captain be with us?"

Lestor smiled and turned back around. "He's got better things to do, Lieutenant. Proceed with the launch."

"Aye, ma'am."

The *Weippe* slowly edged away from the space dock and picked up speed as it cruised past the other, newer starships. Her dark gray hull, still smudged with black scoring from her previous missions, contrasted sharply with the clean, light gray starships she passed.

"Bridge to Commander Vance."

"Go ahead, Number One," Vance answered while chewing his egg.

"We have cleared the docks, sir."

"Outstanding. Set course for the Arcab system."

Lestor motioned to Helm and then replied. "Aye, sir. Setting course for Arcab."

Commander Vance's voice piped through the intercom. "Senior officers to the wardroom in thirty minutes, please."

"Aye, sir," Lestor answered. She wrapped her fingers around the brown leather arm pads of the captain's chair and sat up straight. She knew they would escort a train of tanker ships from Arkab to Selene. It would be a cakewalk mission. It was good to be back to normal.

Starship Series Reading Order

Corvette – First Command

Corvette – Seer of the Black Star

Corvette – Pirate's Lair

Destroyer – Declo Demons

Destroyer – The Mutineers

Destroyer – Letting Go

Explorer – New Horizons

Explorer – Searchers

Explorer – Destiny

www.ingramcontent.com/pod-product-compliance
Lightning Source LLC
Chambersburg PA
CBHW022049050726
47591CB00002B/466